Claire hate...

"You've been ... Roger, and alre... ... playing games," Claire fumed at ... couple.

"We just wanted to. . ."

"I know exactly what you wanted to do, Gloria. However, let me set the record straight for you, Jake," she said, glaring across the table. "If you have any intention of marriage or, for that matter, any type of commitment, you've been introduced to the wrong person."

A sharp elbow landed in Claire's ribs just as she completed the statement.

"Whaaat?" Claire asked, rubbing her side while looking at Gloria. "He might as well know where I stand! If you and Roger are intent on playing these matchmaking games, your prey should know the rules," she continued, as though Jake weren't present and hearing the conversation.

"Claire. . ." Gloria began.

"I can speak for myself, Gloria," Jake replied, his azure blue eyes locked on Claire. "You need not worry, Claire. You've just met the man of your dreams—I'm thirty-five years old, never been married, and never intend to make *that* mistake. So it would appear we have at least one thing in common, wouldn't you say?"

JUDITH MCCOY MILLER was chosen favorite new author in the Heartsong series, and her historical novels have ranked high among readers. In her first contemporary novel, Judith drew on events in her own life to make the story come alive. She makes her home in Kansas with her family.

HEARTSONG PRESENTS

Books by Judith McCoy Miller
HP223—Threads of Love
HP244—Woven Threads

A Trusting
Heart

Judith McCoy Miller

Heartsong Presents

With love and thanks to my mother, Gladys McCoy, whose resilient existence has been a living example of the truths professed in Ephesians 5:20 and Psalm 30:5.

A note from the author:
I love to hear from my readers! You may correspond with me by writing:　　　　**Judith McCoy Miller**
Author Relations
PO Box 719
Uhrichsville, OH 44683

ISBN 1-57748-395-2

A TRUSTING HEART

Cover illustration by Jocelyne Bouchard.

PRINTED IN THE U.S.A.

prologue

Jake Lindsey made a left turn and steered his car into the lime-stone-walled cemetery. His wife, Claire, sat beside him on the beige, leather-upholstered seat of their white Honda Accord. Silently, they drove along the narrow gravel road, both of them watching for the gray marble statue of a little boy balancing an urn upon his head. In the spring and summer, the pitcher spewed a steady stream of water on the surrounding triangular flower bed. In autumn and winter, the flowers were replaced by fallen leaves, and the splashing water ceased to flow. Throughout the year, however, the statue served as a marker, dividing the roadway into separate sections of the cemetery.

"Turn left, here," Claire quietly instructed, breaking the silence.

"I know," Jake replied, giving her a slight smile and nodding his head.

"Habit," Claire said. "You know me. I've always got to give directions."

He said nothing, but took one hand from the steering wheel and laid it on top of hers. "After all these years, I wouldn't know what to do if you stopped telling me how and where to drive," he said, squeezing her hand.

"I'm okay, Jake," she said, giving him a warm smile. "Really, I am. God has brought us so far since this time last year."

He returned her smile and pulled the car as far off the gravel road as possible. "Better put your coat on. It's windy," he warned as he opened her car door.

Together they walked to the back of the vehicle, and Claire stood waiting as Jake removed a huge hanging basket containing Christmas greens, holly, and red poinsettias. A large, red-and-green plaid, weatherproof ribbon was securely wired to the top of the container. Carrying the floral arrangement in one hand, Jake positioned his arm around Claire's waist and led her toward Michelle's grave. Without saying anything further, Jake pulled the wire cutters from his overcoat, removed the hanging basket they had suspended above the grave several months earlier, and then placed it on the ground. Picking up the new basket, he secured the wire hook on the heavy metal base and took the fresh piece of wire that Claire handed him. She watched as he meticulously rotated the wire, bending and turning until it met his exacting specifications.

"How's that?" he asked. "I think it's good and secure," he continued as if in answer to her unasked question.

"It looks great," she replied, her eyes drifting downward to the mauve-colored headstone they had chosen. An angel in flight was carved into the upper-left corner, symbolizing Michelle's emancipation from her impaired physical body into the sovereign freedom of eternity with God. A simple verse was engraved below her name: "Think of her as living in the hearts of those she touched, for nothing loved is ever lost, and she was loved so much." That unambiguous phrase represented the emotions of everyone who had ever developed a bond with their sweet Michelle. And it was those people, plus an abiding faith in God, that had kept Claire and Jake afloat during the grief-ridden months that followed Michelle's death. When there were no words to say and no deeds that lent solace, they relied upon the great Comforter, resting in the knowledge that their child was safe in His arms.

There had been times, especially for Claire, when even God's comfort had seemed insufficient to assuage her grief. In many respects, it appeared that Claire's mourning mirrored the struggle of Michelle's life—insurmountable. But Michelle had risen to the challenge of her life, and Claire acknowledged that she herself could do no less. Amazingly, the pain had slowly diminished and, over a period of time, was replaced by a genuine peace and contentment. Claire now accepted the fact that she would always miss Michelle, but she also permitted herself to find joy in releasing her child to a better life.

The cold December air stirred the pine trees standing vigil over the row of graves. Claire seated herself on the white wrought-iron bench that Jake had placed under a pine flourishing near Michelle's headstone and pulled the collar of her wool, hunter-green coat high around her neck.

Where has all the time gone? she thought. *It seems like only yesterday when I was arguing with Gloria that I didn't want her setting up blind dates and meddling in my life.*

one

"For the third time, Gloria, I don't want to go out to dinner with you and Roger," Claire Winslow stated, the irritation in her voice unmistakable.

"Honestly, Claire, you'd think I was suggesting you do something illegal, instead of trying to pry you out of this house for a little adult conversation and companionship," Gloria replied.

"I was already going to go out for adult conversation and companionship—with *you*, remember?" Claire retorted, her green eyes flashing.

"I know, I know. If you want me to tell Roger to forget it, I will. It's just that he's been on temporary duty assignment for three weeks, and I didn't know he'd be back tonight when we made our plans. . ."

"Gloria! Go out to dinner with him. Enjoy yourself, but leave me out of it. I'd feel like the fifth wheel tagging along."

"No! I told Roger that I had promised you we were going to dinner tonight. He insisted I bring you. Besides, he said there would probably be some other people dropping by."

"Dropping by? What does 'dropping by' mean? And who are these other people?" Claire asked, suddenly suspicious.

Gloria Vargas and Claire Winslow had become friends four years earlier while working at the same law office. It was a small practice, just two attorneys plus Gloria, who was a legal secretary; Claire, who was a legal assistant; and the receptionist, Josie, who had just graduated from high school. Although she was a sweet girl, Josie's age precluded her from having much in common with the other two women.

When Glenn Winslow, Claire's husband, had died two

years earlier while on a vacation in Colorado, it was Gloria who met her at the airport upon her arrival home, never leaving her side until Claire's mother arrived. Claire and Gloria had a strong friendship, although they didn't agree on everything. One of their primary disagreements arose over the fact that Gloria was determined that Claire should begin dating again. Consequently, whenever Gloria used terminology such as "dropping by," Claire's antennae went up. Claire had been easy to dupe the first few times Gloria tried her hand at matchmaking. But throughout the past few months, Claire had learned most of her friend's tricks.

At twenty-nine, Gloria was five years Claire's junior and had never been married, although she thought it was in Claire's best interest to once again tie the knot. In contrast, Claire was just as sure that she should remain single. After steadfastly avowing that marriage was not for her, Gloria was now blissfully in love with Roger and was even more determined that Claire should once again find someone with whom to share her life.

"You know, Claire, you're the most skeptical person I've ever known. Roger said that some of the guys from his company mentioned they might be at the Circle Restaurant tonight too. That's what I meant when I said 'dropping by.' You're making a mountain out of a molehill. I wouldn't have even said anything except that you didn't want to be a threesome. Please say you'll go."

"You're beginning to sound like a whiny two-year-old," Claire said as she poured a cup of coffee and sat down across from her friend at the kitchen table. "Sure is a pretty evening, isn't it?" she asked, watching the two young neighbor children next door playing in a sprinkler. Their squeals of delight, along with the rat-a-tat-tat of the turning sprinkler, reverberated across the short distance and through the screened kitchen windows.

"Yeah, it is. You're going to get all melancholy on me if you sit here staring at those kids. Come on, Claire. I'll give you fifteen minutes to repair your makeup and fix your hair, or I'm going to call Roger and we'll physically drag you to the restaurant."

"All right, but I need at least an hour. I want to relax a few more minutes, and then I'll get ready. Pick me up around seven o'clock."

"You sure drive a hard bargain," Gloria said, giving her friend a grin. "I'll be back at seven, and you'd better be ready to go! I won't take any excuses," she warned as she walked out the screen door, allowing it to slam closed after her.

Claire watched as the petite brunette jogged down the driveway to her car, her bronze complexion accented by the creamy white silk blouse she was wearing. "How can anyone look so good all the time?" Claire murmured as her friend slipped behind the wheel of her sleek red Chevy.

It was exactly seven o'clock when Gloria came to a halt in the driveway and tooted the horn. Claire shook her head as she pulled the front door closed behind her. Wearing a pair of black slacks and pale gold blouse that accented the blond highlights in her light brown hair, Claire walked toward the car. The two women presented a striking contrast. Claire was seven inches taller with a much more curvaceous figure, light brown hair, green eyes, and fair complexion. Gloria, on the other hand, at a mere five feet, had a "little-boy" petite figure, short black hair, dark eyes, and bronze complexion.

Claire and Gloria were almost as different in their religious beliefs as they were in appearance. Throughout their friendship, they had prayed for each other, and both of them loved God. But their methods of worship differed as much as their lives. Neither was willing to compromise her beliefs, nor did the other expect it. Yet the bond of Christian love ran deep between the two women.

"I was watching for you—you didn't have to lay on the horn and alert the whole neighborhood," Claire remarked, giving her friend a teasing smile.

"I don't think those few little toots were enough to alert the whole neighborhood, but if you don't shake a leg, I'll see what I can do," she called out the rolled-down car window.

"Don't do me any favors," Claire replied, opening the car door and sliding onto the seat.

"Where's Roger?"

"He's going to meet us there. He said he'd hitch a ride with one of the other guys," Gloria answered casually.

The Circle was a favorite restaurant in the small military town adjacent to Fort Riley and was usually packed on weekends. By the time they pulled into the parking lot, Claire was already dreading the long wait for a table and the thought of being surrounded by throngs of loud, gregarious people she didn't know.

"Don't even think about it," Gloria said, eyeing her friend.

"What does that mean?" Claire asked.

"I know what you're thinking," Gloria replied.

"You don't have any idea what I'm thinking," Claire rebutted, staring out the car window as they pulled alongside another car in the parking lot.

"You're wishing you were at home and you're devising some outlandish plan so that I'll take you," Gloria smugly answered.

"Not quite—but close," she admitted as she opened the car door.

"Come on, it'll be fun. Visiting, good food. . ."

"Right! People I don't know, calories I don't need, conversations I'm not interested in—it'll be great fun."

"Now who's sounding like a whiny two-year-old?" Gloria asked, but not waiting for an answer. "Roger! Over here," she waved, jumping up and down to attract his attention.

It took no time for Roger to spot Gloria. Petite or not, she could make herself heard. And the minute Roger caught sight of them, he came bolting across the room and swept

Gloria into a giant bear hug. Not sure how to handle what seemed an extremely awkward situation, Claire attempted to disassociate herself from the two of them as they kissed and embraced. It was obvious to everyone in the restaurant that they were delighted the three-week hiatus in their relationship was now over.

"Hi, Claire," Roger offered when he finally came up for air.

"Hi, Roger. Did you have a table for us over there?" Claire inquired, desperately wanting to move out of the group gathered at the front of the restaurant who were obviously enjoying the couple's reunion.

"We've got a great table," he advised, weaving through the crowd toward a long table where several couples were seated, along with a solitary man.

"Who is *he*?" Claire hissed in Gloria's ear. "He'd better have a wife or girlfriend in the bathroom," she continued when Gloria didn't answer.

"Hey, Jake—this is Claire Winslow. Claire—meet Jake Lindsey," Roger stated, introducing the man seated across the table from Claire.

Jake nodded and rose from his chair until the women were seated, his six-foot, three-inch frame towering over the rest of them. Claire said nothing.

"So, how you been, Jake?" Gloria inquired in an obvious attempt at conversation.

"I've been fine. It's nice to see you again, Gloria. It's nice to meet you, Claire," he stated, forcing her to reply.

"Why?" Claire asked.

"Why, what?"

"*Why* is it nice to meet me? Did you *know* you were going to meet me? Because I didn't know I was going to meet *you*, Jake. It is *Jake*, isn't it? It seems that Roger and Gloria have been busy attempting to run my life again. You've been back in town less than twenty-four hours, Roger, and already the two of you are back to playing games," Claire fumed at the surprised couple.

"We just wanted to. . ."

"I know exactly what you wanted to do, Gloria. However, let me set the record straight for you, Jake," she said, glaring across the table. "If you have any intention of marriage or, for that matter, any type of commitment, you've been introduced to the wrong person."

A sharp elbow landed in Claire's ribs just as she completed the statement.

"Whaaat?" Claire asked, rubbing her side while looking at Gloria. "He might as well know where I stand! If you and Roger are intent on playing these matchmaking games, your prey should know the rules," she continued, as though Jake weren't present and hearing the conversation.

"Claire. . ." Gloria began.

"I can speak for myself, Gloria," Jake replied, his azure blue eyes locked on Claire. "You need not worry, Claire. You've just met the man of your dreams—I'm thirty-five years old, never been married, and never intend to make *that* mistake. So it would appear we have at least one thing in common, wouldn't you say?"

Claire was relieved when the waiter appeared at that very moment. "I'll have the dinner buffet, coffee, and my check is separate," she told the young man. Nodding, he continued around the table taking orders and finally arrived across the table beside Jake.

"I'll have the dinner buffet, iced tea, and my check is separate also—unless you'd like to pay for it," he said, looking up and catching Claire staring at him.

A deep blush began to rise, and she could feel the heat climbing upward into her cheeks. "I'll allow him to pay for his own," she replied, turning to talk with Gloria.

"I think they're into a pretty deep conversation at the moment," Jake commented, nodding toward Gloria and Roger.

"Now me—I'd be happy to talk to you," he offered, giving her a broad smile that caused the small lines at the edges of his eyes to crinkle.

"Where did you get a tan like that, this time of year?" Claire ventured, surprised at his deep bronze shade before summer's arrival.

"It's called *desert tan*," he replied, once again giving her an engaging smile, his blue eyes twinkling. "I was in California from January through the end of March for training. It's one of those added bonuses of being in the Army that I could do without."

That explained not only the tan, but also the pronounced sun streaks blended throughout his brown, wavy hair. Although his hair conformed to the usual short military cut, there was a definite curl that defied being totally eliminated. His broad shoulders and muscular build were evidence of his profession as a well-trained soldier.

"I think I could live with a job that sent me to California for the winter without too many complaints," Claire replied as she took a sip of her warm coffee. "Think I should have ordered iced tea. Appears the waiter's going to be too busy to keep the coffee hot enough for my taste."

Jake merely nodded at her remark.

"So tell me what it's like to spend the winter on the sunny beaches of California," Claire urged.

"I wouldn't know. I said I spent the winter in California, but I'm afraid I didn't see any sunny beaches. We were training at Fort Irwin. Know anything about Fort Irwin?" he asked, without waiting for an answer. "It's in the desert—one of those really *plum* assignments you hope never comes your way. However, my name seems to be permanently recorded on someone's Fort Irwin winter-fun list."

"It can't be all that bad—at least it's warm, right?"

"Oh it's warm in the daytime, all right! The reflection of the sun beating on that sand produces unbelievable heat.

Then once the sun goes down in the evening, you're plagued with nights so cold that sometimes it snows. But believe it or not, the sun rises the next morning and you're suffering from the heat all over again. And that's just a *couple* of the reasons I'd be glad to do without California in the winter," he answered while gesturing at the waiter to bring Claire a glass of iced tea.

Claire couldn't help smiling at his remarks. He had a funny way of telling stories and a casual easiness about him that was beginning to make her feel comfortable in his presence.

"Thank you," she said to the waiter as he deposited the glass of tea beside her dinner plate. "And thank you for ordering it," she said, looking over at Jake.

"You're quite welcome. I'll just have to make sure he puts it on your bill and not mine," he answered with a chuckle.

"I'll double-check, to be sure," she countered, opening a packet of artificial sweetener and dumping it into the glass.

"Sure you wouldn't rather have some sugar instead of the imitation stuff? Didn't Congress ban that because it causes cancer in rats? It can't possibly be good for *you* if it's killing off rats," Jake cautioned, offering her the sugar. "I'd hate to see you become a casualty," he continued, giving her a teasing grin.

"I'll wait until they prove something a little more definite," Claire replied, returning his smile while ignoring the sugar.

"Roger wants to know if you two would like to go over to the Abbotts' house after dinner. They're having a welcome home party," Gloria whispered to Claire.

"Not me," Claire replied. "You can ask Jake to go along, but I'm afraid that might turn into something that doesn't interest me. Don't you remember the last party you attended at the Abbotts'?" Claire continued, keeping her voice low enough that the others couldn't hear their conversation.

"I'm driving tonight, so I don't have to worry. If they start drinking, I can leave," Gloria retorted.

"Suit yourself, but I'm not going," Claire firmly replied.

"What's the big secret?" Jake inquired.

"Roger was wondering if you and Claire wanted to go to a party at the Abbotts' house after dinner," Gloria said, obviously intending to ignore Claire's refusal.

"Doesn't sound appealing to me. I never have liked those 'home' parties the wives throw when their husbands get back from training. Besides, I think I'll call it an early night," he said while rising from his chair. "Anyone else ready to try out the buffet?"

"I am. You and Roger coming?" Claire asked Gloria, while giving her a smug grin. "Didn't work, did it?" she whispered in Gloria's ear just as they reached the buffet line.

"If you're not interested in going to the Abbotts', how about going back over to Claire's house for coffee when we leave?" Gloria asked Jake as he was helping himself to a generous serving of potatoes and gravy.

"Sure—that would be okay," he replied, continuing down the buffet line.

Feigning an inability to decide upon an entree, Claire waited until Jake was a short distance away. "Just what do you thing you're doing, Gloria?" she asked through clenched teeth.

"Giving you and Jake an opportunity to get to know each other. You seem determined to get away from him as soon as possible, so I thought I'd better get things turned in the right direction. If you don't want to go to the Abbotts' party—then it's coffee and conversation at your house!"

It wasn't often that Gloria got the best of her friend, and had Claire listened to her instincts, it wouldn't have happened tonight. Now Gloria had pushed her into the position of either treating Jake as rudely as she had earlier or taking them all home and entertaining. Neither idea appealed to her, and she silently vowed that next Friday night would find her curled up on the couch with a good book.

"You want to ride with me?" Jake asked as the four of them walked to the parking lot outside the restaurant.

"Go ahead, Claire. Roger doesn't have his car, so he's riding with me," Gloria instructed with a smug smile of her own.

Claire acted as though she hadn't noticed. "We'll follow you," Claire replied, allowing Jake to escort her toward his car. Lowering herself inside, she seated herself and leaned across to unlock the door of the small sports car.

"What is this thing, anyway? I feel like I'm sitting on the ground," Claire asked as Jake turned the ignition key and revved the motor.

"It's a Datsun. I bought it right after I got back from Germany. Nothing I love more than a sports car. As to sitting on the ground, you eventually get used to it," he replied. Pulling out of the parking lot behind Gloria, he adroitly shifted through the gears as they moved onto the highway. "I had a pretty little blue Ford Capri while I was stationed in Germany, but I sold it right before I came back to the States. I sure miss driving on the autobahn—ever been to Europe?"

"No, I'm afraid I haven't made it east of Philadelphia or west of Denver," she replied, watching his obvious enjoyment as he wove through traffic.

"Bet you'd love it—course there's no place like the United States, but it's fun traveling overseas. At least in peace time," he added.

"From that remark, I'd guess you've been to Vietnam."

"Yep. Made somebody's list for those tours, too."

"You went more than once?" she asked, surprised by his answer.

"I had the undeniable pleasure of three tours, although Uncle Sam designated those assignments pretty carefully. There were actually regulations prohibiting three tours, so instead of a full tour, they sent me on temporary duty assignment the third time. I had to stay for only nine months instead of eleven," he said, shaking his head and giving a small laugh.

"Didn't you ever question your orders? I mean, why you had to go three times and others didn't have to go at all?"

"Nope! It's part of the job. I knew when I made the Army a career that combat was part of the deal. Course I didn't realize coming back into the United States would be like entering another war zone. I think that part was harder than all the time I spent in Vietnam."

"I don't envy you," she replied, knowing that many of the returning soldiers had suffered severely while in Vietnam, as well as being treated disgracefully by American citizens when they returned to the States.

He grew silent and stared straight ahead as though deep in thought. "Well, that's enough of that! I don't want to throw you into total depression," he said, smiling. "By the way, how come we're following Gloria to *your* house? Afraid you'd forget your way home?" he asked, giving her a knowing grin.

"I wasn't sure Gloria would show up. I know she wants to go to that party. . ."

"And you wanted to be sure you didn't end up with a stranger camped on your front doorstep," he said, completing her statement.

"Something like that," she honestly replied. "Are you offended?" she inquired, though not sure that his answer really mattered.

"Nah. It takes more than that to insult me!"

two

Racing in the front door, Claire dropped the two bags of groceries on the kitchen table and grabbed the phone.

"Hello," she answered in a breathless voice.

"Been out jogging?" asked the voice at the other end of the line.

"Who is this?"

"Jake! Jake Lindsey—we had dinner last Friday night, and I came to your house for coffee afterward. Ring any bells?"

"How did you get my phone number? It's unlisted," Claire abruptly replied.

"Gloria came to the rescue. Now that is one girl I wouldn't want for an enemy—look what she does for her friends," he said, laughing at his own joke.

"Listen, I just got in from shopping, and I need to get these groceries put away before they defrost all over the table. I'll talk to you some other time," she stated, calling an abrupt halt to his bantering.

"Whoa! Hold on a minute. I wondered if you'd like to do something this weekend. I've tried to call several times this week, but you're a hard lady to find at home."

"No, thanks. I'm going to be busy. I've really got to go," she responded and promptly hung up the phone without saying good-bye.

Approximately thirty minutes later, the ringing telephone summoned Claire from the relaxing bubble bath she'd been promising herself all week. She was tempted to let it ring, but the thought that it might be a call about her daughter, Michelle, caused her to veto that idea. Rising out of the sudsy, herbal-scented water, she wrapped herself in a huge terrycloth robe, slid her wet feet into a pair of blue thongs, and padded across the pale gold bedroom carpet.

"Hello," she answered in a voice filled with more irritation than she'd intended.

"Still unloading the groceries?"

"Oh, for goodness sake. It's *you* again."

"You sure know how to overwhelm a guy with your enthusiasm. If I didn't know better, I'd think that you were irritated that I called back," he replied.

"I already told you I'm busy this weekend, and your call forced me out of the bathtub. So, to be perfectly honest with you, I *am* irritated you called back," she stated.

"Tell you what—I'll let you get back to that bath. You just tell me a good time to call, and that will solve my interruptions," he suggested.

"There's no reason to call back. I've already said all there is to say."

"I thought we had quite a bit to talk about last Friday night. I really would like to get to know you better—absolutely no strings attached. Like I told you, I'm not interested in any commitments either," he continued, obviously not willing to hang up.

"Half an hour," she answered and slammed down the phone. "The water's already cold," she muttered under her breath as she turned on the hot water faucet and stepped back into the tub.

"Hello," Claire dispassionately answered when the telephone rang exactly one half-hour later.

"I hope I'm not taking you away from anything important this time," Jake replied.

"Nothing but writing checks, washing dishes, and general housecleaning."

"You should be thanking me for calling. Look at what I've saved you from," he jokingly responded.

There was a deafening silence at the other end of the line.

"You still there?" he asked.

"Jake, you called me. What is it you wanted to talk about?"

"Everything. Nothing. I just wanted to talk to you. Are you sure you couldn't squeeze in a little time this weekend?"

"I'm afraid not. I've got a bizillion things to do."

"Couldn't I do some of them with you? Help out or something?" he asked.

"I don't think they'd appeal to you."

"Well, just try me," he encouraged her. "What are you doing on Saturday?"

"Mowing the yard and planting some flowers in front of the house. If I'm lucky, I'll also get a few tomato plants and green onions in the ground. Sound like anything you're interested in?" she asked with a hint of sarcasm in her voice.

"Do you serve breakfast?"

"Only *after* the work's done," she stated, surprised at his question.

"What time should I be there, and do you want me to pick up the tomato plants?"

"Are you serious?" she asked, realizing that he wasn't going to be put off.

"Sure, I'm serious. I'll see you at eight o'clock Saturday morning. You buying the tomatoes, or am I?"

"I'll buy the tomatoes," she answered.

"Good enough. Don't forget about breakfast! See you on Saturday," he said with a lilt in his voice and then hung up the phone.

Claire stood staring at the receiver, stunned at how easily he had manipulated himself into her weekend.

⁓

Jake arrived at eight o'clock on Saturday morning dressed in a pair of jeans, a faded olive drab T-shirt, and a pair of old combat boots.

Claire couldn't help grinning when she looked at his feet.

"Combat boots to mow the yard? Around here, most of us do yard work in tennis shoes."

"I had a friend that lost a couple toes one summer when he was mowing the grass. He was barefooted. Ever since then, I've worn boots when I mow the yard. Laugh if you want, but I'd rather have warm feet than take a chance losing my toes," he replied seriously.

"I'm sorry. . ." she began.

"No need to be. I've still got all my toes," he joked, obviously realizing that his response made her feel uncomfortable. "Tell me where the mower is, and I'll get started."

It was eleven o'clock by the time they were in the kitchen, eating scrambled eggs and toasted English muffins.

"This is great," Jake complimented as Claire poured him a second cup of strong Colombian coffee.

"I'd say it's the least I could do after a morning of hard work. It would have taken me a couple more hours without your help."

"That works out well for me then, doesn't it?"

"Why is that?" Claire questioned.

"It gives you a couple hours to spend with me," he said, giving her a wink.

"I really do have plans for this afternoon, Jake," she replied.

"I'll bet I could help out if you'd let me."

"It's really nothing I need help with. I'm going to spend the afternoon with my daughter."

"I didn't know you had any kids," he stated, a question evident in his eyes.

"Didn't Roger tell you I'm a widow?" she asked.

"Yes. He said your husband died a couple years ago, but he didn't say you had kids."

"I don't have *kids*. I have one daughter. Her name is Michelle," she told him.

"How old is she?"

"Twelve."

"Twelve? Is she living with her grandparents or something?" he asked, obviously confused.

"No. She's profoundly retarded and lives in a group home with two other girls who are equally disabled."

"Who takes care of them?" he inquired.

"They attend day classes at a school for the developmentally disabled during the day and return back to their house in the evening. They're cared for by professional staff around the clock," she answered, wishing that the conversation would take a different course.

"So where's this group home located?"

"It's about thirty miles east of here. I dislike the distance, but professional help for Michelle was my most important consideration. It was probably the hardest decision I ever had to make," she quietly remarked. *Why did I tell him that?* she immediately thought to herself, angry that she'd divulged something so private to a stranger.

"I can't even begin to imagine," he replied in a somber voice.

"Well, I think I'd better get these dishes cleared away and start getting ready to leave town," she said, forcing herself to sound cheerful.

"How about if I tag along?" he requested.

"I don't think so. But I do appreciate all your help this morning," she added.

"I'd be glad to do the driving," he cajoled, giving her an engaging grin.

"Please don't push me on this issue, Jake. If there's anything in this world I'm decisive about, it's issues regarding Michelle."

"I think I believe you," he said, obviously noting the determined set of her jaw. "Could I at least get an okay to call you tomorrow? How about brunch or the zoo? I love zoos—or we could go see the buffalo at Fort Riley. What do you say?"

"I go to church on Sunday mornings, and I told Gloria I'd

give her a call tomorrow afternoon. We had tentatively planned to do some shopping," she replied.

"I'll give Gloria a call while you're gone this afternoon and see if she'd mind giving up her shopping trip," he ventured.

"How about church, Jake? Do you attend anywhere?" she asked.

"No, you know what with moving around and all, I never got into that. My folks sent me on Sunday mornings when I was little—I think so they could sleep in and I wouldn't bother them," he said, laughing nervously at his last remark.

"Do you move more often than most of the soldiers stationed out here?" she asked.

"Well, probably not. I seem to go TDY—that's temporary duty assignment—quite a bit, but I've been attached to Fort Riley for three years now," he responded.

"Seems like plenty of time to find a church home. We have quite a few military families in our church. They add so much to the congregation. Most of them have belonged to lots of churches and bring fresh ideas and new blood into the membership. Personally, I think they keep us from getting stale. Course, I always hate to see them leave on new assignments, but it seems just about the time one couple is ready to leave, one or two more arrive. You might even know some of them," she stated, with a note of encouragement in her voice.

"So are you inviting me to church tomorrow morning?" he asked, sounding somewhat hesitant.

"Certainly. But, please don't view going to church as a date, okay? I invite lots of people to church, and I sincerely hope that everyone I ask will show up the following Sunday morning," she explained. "It's the Maranatha Fellowship at the corner of Madison and Countryside. Do you know where that is?"

"After three years in this town, I think I know where that is," he replied with a smile. "What time does it begin?"

"Ten-thirty. I'll meet you out front," she responded.

"Why don't I just stop by for you? No sense in taking two cars."

"I'll be going earlier. I meet with a prayer group before the ten-thirty service," she explained. "Besides, I may need to stay afterward. It'll be easier if I have my car."

"Will you be able to go out to lunch afterwards? We could take a picnic to the zoo," he offered doggedly.

"I'm afraid not. I hate to seem rude, but I really need to get ready to leave," she said, hoping he would take the hint.

Claire walked him to the back door and watched as he walked toward his car. "I'll wait out front in case you decide to come in the morning," she called after him.

He waved his arm in the air with car keys dangling from his hand, but he didn't respond.

❧

The thirty-mile ride to Michelle's group home gave Claire time to think. It had been a week since her last visit. Sometimes there was an evening when she could manage to squeeze in the trip, but last week there hadn't been. Unfortunately, she always suffered from a gnawing guilt when something occurred to interrupt those regular trips. Not that the staff at the home made her feel guilty—it was merely Claire and her obsession with being a perfect parent to her daughter.

From the time Michelle had been diagnosed as profoundly retarded, Claire had desperately clung to her intense faith in God. Armed with the knowledge that their daughter had been born with extensive brain damage, Claire believed that God's divine plan would one day be revealed to them. But until that time, she concluded that there was nothing more important to Michelle than the love and protection of her parents. Glenn had preferred that they take a more detached attitude and plan to institutionalize Michelle at an early age. Consequently there had been many disagreements about

Michelle's care, but it was Claire who generally had the final say.

Sensing Glenn's indifference toward the child and his determination to remain aloof and detached only served to fuel Claire's efforts to gain a modicum of normalcy to their lives.

Initially Glenn had attempted to convince Claire to immediately institutionalize their daughter. It wasn't that Glenn was an ogre; he was simply agreeing with the recommendation of the specialists who had diagnosed their child.

It is the most humane thing for all retarded children, the doctors had said. *The institutions can give her the things you can't. The two of you can get on with your lives—have other children.*

Claire had resisted, not sure the doctors were correct in their diagnosis and hoping there was a doctor who would give her encouragement. Seeking medical answers wherever they traveled, Claire never hesitated to call Junction City for a referral from their family physician. She had called him from the East Coast while visiting her parents, from the upper Midwest while visiting her brother, from the Southeast while visiting her sister, and from any other large city they visited. But the doctor appointments were futile, eventually reinforcing Claire's earlier conclusion that the most important things she could offer her daughter were love and protection.

Then, during a particularly difficult episode of pneumonia when she was a year old, Michelle had to be hospitalized. Margie Rayton, an excellent registered nurse, was assigned to Michelle's care and explained to Claire that she, too, was the parent of a brain-damaged daughter. Sometimes, late at night while the other patients slept, Margie would come and visit with Claire. The two of them would commiserate about the futility of seeking help for their daughters. During one of those discussions, Margie had told Claire of a program she'd discovered for "patterning" brain-damaged children, a form of home physical therapy using volunteers; she added that she had already been to Philadelphia to have her daughter evaluated.

Claire had been so excited that evening when Glenn had returned home from work. Her words tumbled all over each other as she attempted to share the information she'd discovered earlier that day. He had been less than enthusiastic, pointing out the expense, the probability that Michelle wouldn't be accepted into their program, the fact the program wasn't even approved by the American Medical Association, and the additional heartbreak when their efforts failed.

She and Glenn had fought bitterly, but Claire won. It had been a tough battle—one in which she was forced to make a concession she later regretted.

❧

"How's my girl doing?" Claire asked as she walked in the front door of the tan, vinyl-sided ranch style house that was now Michelle's home.

"Just great, Mrs. Winslow," Sandra called from the kitchen. "She's in there doing her favorite thing," the woman said, pointing toward the family room.

Claire walked up behind her daughter, whispered in her ear, and then nuzzled her on the neck. Michelle rewarded Claire with one of her joy-filled laughs, her head moving back and forth, which caused her thick brown hair to sway back and forth. Those laughs never ceased to bring a smile to Claire's face.

"Just what are you watching?" she asked her daughter, knowing she wouldn't receive an answer. "Looks like you lucked out, kiddo. Sandra managed to find you some cartoons on a Saturday afternoon, didn't she?"

Claire pulled a chair close to her daughter, sat down, and began watching cartoons with her. When Michelle began to fuss, Claire pulled a hank of yarn out of her purse and ran it across the child's fingers. Immediately, Michelle's fussing ceased and her eyes focused on the yarn, her hands pulling it into tangles, as if working an unknown puzzle.

"You bring her more yarn?" Sandra asked, shaking her head.

"You know, Sandra, I don't see what's wrong with giving her yarn to play with. It's no different from allowing her to watch television. It's her weekend, so why shouldn't she enjoy the things she likes to do?"

"All I know is what they keep telling me at the day facility. They already know she likes the feel of yarn. But 'she needs to develop responses to other tactile stimulation,' so I'm not supposed to give it to her,'" Sandra repeated in the typical sing-song voice the occupational therapist always used with Claire.

"I know, I know—but *you* didn't give it to her. Besides, I'll take it home with me and nobody will be the wiser," Claire told the girl.

"Pretty day out there. You can take her for a walk if you want," Sandra suggested.

"When cartoons are over. She'd rather see them than be outdoors," Claire replied.

"What she wants and what's good for her are two different things," Sandra stated wisely.

"I have no doubt that she gets what's *good* for her all week. When I'm around, she gets to have what she *wants*," Claire retorted.

Sandra turned on her heel and quickly walked out of the room, leaving mother and daughter staring at an ancient rerun of *Daffy Duck*.

"I'm sorry, Sandra," Claire apologized a few minutes later when the aide returned to give Michelle her medicine. "It's just that everything is so regimented. You people need to understand that it gives me pleasure to see her enjoy things. There are so few things I can do to make her happy. How can allowing her to play with that yarn do any harm?" Claire asked, tears streaming down her cheeks.

"Come here," Sandra consoled, pulling Claire into her arms. "It's hard having special children, never having the opportunity to see them mature like other kids. But one thing is certain: that child of yours is loved—nobody around here ever doubts that fact. Now dry your eyes, and take her outdoors for awhile. It'll do you both good!"

three

The next morning Claire stationed herself outside the church at exactly ten-fifteen. When her watch reached ten-forty and service had already begun, she felt certain Jake wasn't going to show. Quietly entering the back of the church, she surveyed the crowd and spotted an empty seat close to the rear of the church.

I wonder why Jake didn't show up, she thought to herself when the service had ended. *I should go home and call him to see if there was a problem,* she thought, though knowing she wouldn't.

That evening as she slipped into a pair of pale green silk pajamas, Claire's thoughts drifted back over the weekend. "I'm surprised I didn't hear from Jake," she murmured, pulling back the ivory eyelet comforter and then turning down the matching sheet.

❧

The following week passed in a flurry, and although Claire was able to squeeze in a trip to see Michelle, there was little time for much else. One of the attorneys was preparing for an automobile negligence trial that would begin the following Monday.

"You working late again tonight?" Josie asked, obviously noting that Gloria and Claire weren't making any move toward leaving and it was already after five o'clock.

"Do the geese fly south in winter?" Gloria asked disgustedly. "We'll probably be working late until this trial is over. If you're smart, you'll get out of here while the gettin' is good," she added.

"You don't have to warn me twice," the younger girl

replied, grabbing her small leather purse and tossing the strap on her shoulder. "See you on Monday. Hope you don't have to spend the whole weekend here!"

"Now there's a pleasant thought! You know if these guys wouldn't procrastinate, thinking their cases are going to settle, the rest of us wouldn't have to put in these long hours," Gloria said as she began typing the jury instructions Claire handed her.

"I'm certain that Dave will have some special instructions, but at least you can get started on those. I'll go see what he's working on and try to find out when we can get out of here," Claire called over her shoulder as she walked toward Dave's office.

Returning a few minutes later, she walked over to Gloria's desk. "You have a choice. You can either stay here tonight until everything is ready or come back tomorrow. He said that if you stick around tonight, it may be pretty late. He hasn't finished dictating his opening statement, and there are at least two or three motions he wants the judge to decide upon before the trial begins. He'll need to dictate those also. It would mean you would have to sit around and wait on him," Claire stated.

"How much have you got left to do?" Gloria asked.

"I need to check our copies of the exhibits and make sure they're in order, and Dave wants me to go through the proposed questions and mark the correlating answers the witnesses gave in their depositions. It will probably take a good eight hours, so I think I'll work a few hours tonight and then come back in the morning. You do whatever you want, though," Claire said.

"I don't want to sit around here waiting on him. I think I'll finish up the jury instructions and call it a day. What time are you coming in tomorrow?" Gloria asked.

"Probably around nine. I hope that we can get out of here by noon or one o'clock at the latest."

"Hey, you heard anything from Jake this week?" Gloria asked.

"Where did that question come from? I thought we were talking about work," Claire responded, artfully dodging the question.

"It's the weekend, and I just happened to think about it. So have you or not?"

"Nope. You know all there is to know. I think my invitation to church took care of Jake Lindsey," Claire replied.

"You may be right—you sure know how to weed 'em out! Tell him you have absolutely no interest in commitment, *allow* him to do your yard work on Saturday, and invite him to church on Sunday," Gloria said, laughing. "You probably won't ever hear from him again. Too bad—Roger says he's a nice guy."

"I'm not looking for a guy, Gloria. I keep telling you that, but you just won't listen."

"Right! I keep forgetting—*you* don't need anybody," Gloria retorted and turned back to her typing.

A half-hour later, she piled the neatly typed stack of papers on the corner of her desk. "Those are done. See you tomorrow," Gloria said, removing her purse from the bottom drawer of her desk.

"You're upset with me, aren't you?" Claire asked.

"No, I'm not upset. I just don't understand you. See you in the morning," Gloria answered, walking out the door.

⁂

By Monday morning they were ready for trial. Claire knew the week would be hectic, all day in the courtroom to assist Dave and then back to the office at five o'clock to perform damage control and get ready for the next day. She dreaded the long hours but enjoyed trial work. However, since Dave and Lyle won more cases than most trial attorneys their age, the case load had become increasingly heavier and the trials closer together. In fact, there didn't seem to be much time to recuperate in between anymore.

By late Thursday afternoon they had presented their case, and the defendant would be through early Friday morning. All that remained were summations to the jury and waiting upon a decision. Claire was glad that Dave had finished writing his summation the night before. Gloria had already typed it, and he could spend the evening doing his memorization. Claire would be able to leave by six o'clock.

"You won't know what to do with yourself, getting a good night's sleep," Gloria commented as the two of them left the office that evening.

"I ought to drive over and see Michelle, but I'm so tired," Claire replied as she got into her car.

"You need to get some rest. You can see her this weekend," Gloria replied sternly.

"Okay, okay. Think I'll have a bite to eat and treat myself to a long, hot bubble bath."

"Now, that sounds like a smart idea. See you tomorrow."

"See ya," Claire called, driving out of the parking lot.

Pulling into the one-car garage attached to the house, Claire grabbed the water hose and dragged it to the back of the house without stopping to go inside. "These poor tomato plants," she muttered aloud. "If they don't get some water, I'll never see a tomato this summer." Hooking up the hose, she turned on the water then walked back to the garage, retrieved her purse from the car, and went inside. Checking the freezer, she stood peering into its depths for a few minutes and then slammed the door. *A tuna salad sandwich sounds fine,* she thought, deciding she didn't want to cook anything.

A large glass of milk and tuna salad sandwich later, she returned outside, turned off the water, and disconnected the hose. Too tired to worry about taking the hose back into the garage, she allowed it to remain snaked among the tomatoes. The ringing of the telephone caused her to rush back into the house.

"Hello," she breathlessly answered.

"Jogging again?" came the voice from the other end.

"Jake?" she inquired, pleasantly surprised to hear his voice.

"The one and only," he blithely responded.

"Where have you been?" she asked, without thinking.

"Does that mean you've missed me?"

"No! It means you were driving me nuts for a couple days and then dropped out of sight like you never existed," she replied, suddenly defensive.

"Oh, come on, admit it—you missed me," he teased.

"I haven't had time to miss you, and even if I had, I wouldn't have!"

"You want to run that by me one more time? I'm sure your thoughts were coherent, but they lost something in the spoken word."

"I said—oh, never mind. What do you want?"

"There you go with that attitude again. I'm just going to ignore it. I've been trying to call you for a couple nights, but you must be keeping late hours. Hope I don't have some unknown competition."

"Is there some particular reason why you're calling, or is it just for the pleasure of harassing me?" she asked, a bit of an edge to her voice.

"Sounds like you're in a bad mood. Want some company? Be glad to come over and cheer you up," he offered.

"The last thing I want is company. For your information, I've been working late every night as well as on the weekend," she replied.

"How about this weekend? Could I interest you in that trip to the zoo?"

"I didn't see you at church a couple of weeks ago," she replied, intentionally not answering his question.

"Probably because I wasn't there. I got sick Saturday night and was in bed until Monday," he told her.

"I see. Sounds like sleeping sickness to me."

"It wasn't sleeping sickness; it was sick as in *throw-up* sickness," he replied.

"Well, if you really had the flu, I apologize."

"So does that mean you'll go to the zoo with me on Saturday?"

"I haven't seen Michelle all week. I'm going to see her on Saturday."

"Doesn't she like the zoo?" he asked.

"Sometimes. Sometimes it doesn't appeal to her; it just depends on how she's feeling."

"Sounds like she inherited her mother's attitude problem," he jibed.

Silence reigned at Claire's end of the line.

"Did that remark offend you? I really wasn't trying to offend you. Just attempting to lift your spirits a little."

"Perhaps I'll take you up on that offer. Be here at ten o'clock on Saturday," she replied.

"Yes, ma'am! I almost feel as though I ought to salute," he replied, although he wasn't sure that she heard the remark before clicking the receiver in his ear.

ᕉ

"Ten o'clock sharp," he stated when she opened the front door.

"So it is," she replied, not bothering to invite him inside. "Let's go," she commanded, grabbing her purse and pulling the door closed behind her.

"You'll need to move your car out of the driveway," she directed. "You can either park it on the street or pull it back into the driveway after I get my car out."

"That's okay. I planned on taking my car," he told her.

"*Jake*! You have a sports car that holds two people. We need space for Michelle *and* a specially built wheelchair that is hard to get into most average-sized vehicles," she responded as if instructing a schoolboy.

"Guess I wasn't thinking," he said, giving her a weak smile.

"I'm sure you'll be thinking about a lot of things before this trip is over," she responded, walking away from him and into the garage.

"You want me to drive?" he asked, walking to the driver's side of her vehicle.

"No, I prefer to drive my own car," she told him.

He pulled the door open, slid inside, and slammed the door. Reaching across the seat, he placed his hand on her arm.

"Did I miss something here? I'm sorry I didn't think about the car, but you seem to be slam-dunking me every time I open my mouth. Tell me what I'm doing to irritate you."

She placed her hands on the steering wheel, leaned back, and turned her head toward him. "I guess I owe you an apology. I know this may seem difficult to understand, but in some respects I feel like you're intruding on the special time I spend with my daughter. On the other hand, it's nice to have somebody want to go with me. Plus, I always worry about how people will react to Michelle, so instead of being able to focus on her, I focus on the person with me. Guess that's it in a nutshell. Now, after hearing that little speech, you're welcome to get back in your own car and forget you ever suggested going along. No hard feelings, I promise," she told him.

"Let's go," he answered, pulling the seat belt around his waist.

They rode in silence until they reached the interstate.

"How'd your case end up?" he asked. "Did the white hats win?"

"We won this one, and *I* think we were the white hats," she replied.

"Does that mean there are rare occasions when you admit to representing the black hats?" he asked, simulating disbelief.

"Very rare," she confessed. "We don't handle much criminal defense, so it's easier to say we're the good guys.

Primarily, we handle civil litigation, and one of the attorneys does quite a bit of estate work," she told him.

"No messy divorces and no criminals—that must make it easier to work for attorneys. Personally, I've never been very fond of lawyers."

"Really? Have you had a bad experience?"

"Nope. Just always had a bad taste for them. Seems like they make their living off of other people's problems."

"To some extent, I suppose that's true, but they help resolve problems and somebody's got to do it. I work for two lawyers I consider to be genuinely good men. But there are bad lawyers, just like there are bad soldiers. It's a shame people always lump them together," she continued.

"I suppose you're right," he agreed as she turned off the interstate and braked the car to a stop. "We almost there?" he asked as she pulled away from the stop sign.

"Almost. Getting nervous?"

"A little," he admitted.

"You get ten points for honesty, Jake Lindsey," she replied in a warm voice as she pulled the car into the driveway of Michelle's home.

four

"You seem to be on weekend duty every time I get over here," Claire said, patting Sandra on the back as she and Jake walked by her at the front door.

"Doesn't bother me a bit," Sandra replied. "Got no one at home waiting on me, so I might just as well be here. Who's our new visitor?" she asked, obviously giving Jake a quick appraisal.

"Jake—Jake Lindsey," he replied, reaching across Claire to shake Sandra's extended hand.

"Well now, Shelly girl, what do you think about this? Your Mama finally brought someone along to visit," Sandra said in a childish tone of voice that caused Michelle to giggle.

"Sandra, *please* don't call her Shelly," Claire chastised the stout, middle-aged woman.

"Oh, Claire, she likes to be called Shelly. Don't ya, *Shelly, Shelly, Shelly*," she said, the inflection of her voice once again causing the child to laugh.

"It's not being called Shelly, it's the way you say it that makes her laugh, and you know it," Claire replied while giving the woman an exasperated smile. This was one battle Claire knew she wouldn't win.

"So, Jake—you the kind of guy that deserves the pleasure of this nice lady's company?" Sandra asked, ignoring Claire's glare.

"I'd like to hope so," he replied, appearing uncomfortable with Sandra's direct line of questioning.

"No hoping about it—either you are or you aren't. I've known this lady for about five years, and she doesn't need anymore heartache. So my advice. . ."

"Sandra, if Michelle's ready, I think we're going to go ahead and leave now," Claire interrupted before Sandra could go any further with her lecture.

"She's ready, and I've got her things in the backpack on her wheelchair. You're going to lunch pretty soon, right?" she asked.

"Yes, before we go to the zoo," Claire replied.

"Good, because she hasn't had anything since breakfast. I wanted her to be sure and eat well," Sandra stated, seemingly pleased with herself.

Maneuvering the wheelchair out to the car proved a simple task because everything in and around the house had been made to accommodate the bulky apparatus. However, Jake didn't realize the muscle it would take to break down the large wheelchair after lifting Michelle into the car and arranging her in the seat.

"I don't think I've ever seen a wheelchair quite like that one," he stated, obviously out of breath after the ordeal.

"It was made especially for her. Unfortunately, she's beginning to develop curvature of the spine, and I'm hoping we can avoid surgery by using the chair and a brace part of the time," Claire explained, backing out of the driveway.

"How about lunch at the Village Inn?" Claire asked.

"Sounds fine to me, and I'm ready to eat anytime," Jake responded. "How about you, Michelle?"

"She doesn't talk at all, Jake," Claire explained.

"Oh—sorry. I didn't mean to. . ."

"It's okay, Jake. There are a lot of things you don't know about Michelle. I don't expect you to. You're allowed to ask questions," she stated with a grin. "If you ask anything I don't want to answer, I'll let you know."

Apparently Jake believed her. "Why don't you just *tell* me about Michelle?" he candidly suggested.

"That probably would be easiest," she remarked and then began the story she had told many times. "When Michelle was born, Glenn and I thought everything was fine. We had wanted a little girl very much. Although I'd had some problems with my pregnancy and we had concerns because the doctor didn't arrive at the hospital quickly enough and the baby was held back, we believed everything had turned out perfectly. When I took her for those first few check-ups, the doctor said she was fine. However, I remember questioning him because Michelle seemed to have difficulty taking her bottle. She ate very little, and I'd have to wake her for feedings, or she'd sleep as long as ten hours. Conversely, she'd also go through periods that I explained as 'crying spells' when she would cry until she literally lost her voice. Nothing would appease her, and it would go on day and night until I thought I'd go out of my mind. Still the doctor didn't act alarmed at anything I said. He explained the crying as colic and said she'd awaken if she were hungry."

Jake appeared engrossed by Claire's narrative, occasionally nodding his head.

"When Michelle was about three months old, Glenn and I decided it might be wise to have her checked by a pediatrician. I made the appointment, but Glenn was backlogged at work. We agreed it would be fine for me to go alone. The pediatrician performed a lengthy examination and when he'd finished, he asked if my husband had come along. When I told him that I was alone, he asked me to come back the next morning and to bring Glenn. I knew what he was going to tell us would be unwelcome news and, in retrospect, I marvel that I didn't force him to immediately tell me. Instead, I merely made an appointment for the next morning, left the office, and went home.

"That night, Glenn and I attempted to hide our fear from each other, and early the next morning as we sat in Dr. McNeal's office, he told us that although our daughter was very young to diagnose, it appeared that she had cerebral palsy. Needless to say, I felt like my world was crashing in around me. Glenn and I stared at the doctor in utter disbelief. When he asked if we had any questions, we were both so stunned that we said no. He told us that when we'd had time to reflect upon the news we should come back and talk to him. I remember that we never said a word to each other the whole way home. Both of us cried, but no one said a word. Here we are," she said, pulling into the restaurant parking lot.

Surprised they had already arrived, Jake wished he could hear more of the unfolding circumstances before stopping for lunch.

"I'll get the wheelchair," he offered, reaching out to take the keys.

"Thanks," she replied.

It was nice to have someone else to do some of the heavy-duty lifting that always left her worn out after excursions with her daughter. Watching as Jake removed and reassembled the wheelchair, Claire removed Michelle from the car and lifted her into the chair.

"Here we go," she said to the child, giving her a kiss. "You ready for lunch?" she asked, knowing there would be no answer.

The Village Inn was one of the few restaurants where Claire was always assured that she could get a serving of mashed potatoes and gravy. Decisions about where to eat were always based upon what foods were served that Michelle could swallow. Born with an extremely high gag reflex and unable to chew her food, the choices were limited.

Jake opened the door to the restaurant. After scanning the dining room for several minutes, the waitress found them a table. Claire had learned long ago that sitting in a booth and placing the wheelchair at the end just didn't work. Although being at a table in the center of the dining area wasn't appealing to Claire, she knew it was the easiest seating arrangement when Michelle was going to eat. Unfortunately, the restaurant was quite crowded, and they found themselves in the midst of an obviously hungry lunch crowd.

"She doesn't particularly like being in large group settings such as this," Claire explained when Michelle began to cry. "I didn't realize it would be so jammed," she apologetically stated as Michelle began to cry louder, attracting the attention of the surrounding patrons.

Pulling a small wad of yarn from her purse, Claire held it in front of Michelle's face until the child's eyes focused on the object. Quickly her hands reached toward the object, and the crying ceased.

"I take it there's something about yarn that she likes," Jake commented.

"Yes, although I haven't figured out just what it is," Claire replied, smiling as her daughter played with the object. "Does it bother you?" she asked.

"Playing with the yarn? Why should that bother me?" Jake asked, bringing his eyes back to Claire.

"When people stare. Does it bother you? It appears to me you've been watching for other people's reactions since we entered the restaurant," she observed.

"I'm not sure 'bother' is the right word. It's more that I'm surprised that we seem to be the center of attention. I didn't expect that kind of reaction," he honestly responded.

"I think a lot of it is because most people haven't had much exposure to kids like Michelle. Generally speaking, people seem to be enthralled by the unique and different. Michelle is a rare sight to most folks. Perhaps if enough parents are willing to subject themselves and their children to public scrutiny, the curiosity will decrease," she remarked quietly. "Of course, sometimes that's easier said than done," she quickly added, recalling arguments with Glenn about taking Michelle to public places.

"You're a pretty insightful lady," he complimented as the strains of elevator music drifted throughout the restaurant.

"Believe me, it hasn't come easily. God has really had to

perform a work in me. My immediate reaction when Michelle was diagnosed was one of disbelief, then anger, and then a giant pity party. But God has blessed me for honestly coming before Him with all of those emotions. As time has passed, He's shown me that He has different plans for each of us. Michelle's 'plan' isn't what I had wanted for my daughter, but He has taught me acceptance, and sometimes I truly marvel at the lives she has touched," Claire explained.

Jake nodded but said nothing. Looking toward the waitress who was now standing by their table, he asked, "Have you decided what you'd like?"

"Put ours on a separate bill," Claire told the waitress, nodding her head toward Michelle.

Jake didn't object, although Claire could feel his eyes on her.

"I'll have the fruit plate special and a side order of mashed potatoes, heavy on the gravy, a small glass of milk, and a cup of coffee."

The waitress finished writing, flipped the page in her order book, and turned toward Jake. "What'll it be for you?" she asked without looking up.

"I'll have the chicken-fried steak dinner with French fries, Thousand Island dressing on the salad, and an extra roll. Oh yeah, a large glass of milk with my meal and coffee now," he stated.

Without a word she disappeared, and another waitress appeared with a thermal coffeepot and placed it on the table.

"I planned on paying for dinner, Claire. I won't make scenes in public places if I can avoid them, but I'd like you to allow me to pay for dinner and the zoo," he said as soon as the waitress was out of earshot.

Claire hesitated for a moment before answering. "I really prefer paying my own way. That way there's no feeling of obligation."

She watched Jake stiffen as she made the statement.

"I'm not offering in order to make you feel obligated. I invited you, and I'd like to pay, pure and simple."

"Tell you what—the tickets to the zoo can be your treat, okay?" she asked, still unwilling to allow him to pay for dinner.

"You're in charge," he said, giving her a mock salute along with the hint of a smile.

"That was fast," Claire remarked as the waitress began placing their food on the table. "I thought it would take them forever with this crowd." She pulled a large bib from the backpack and placed it around the child's neck. "She can get a little messy," she explained.

"Anything I can do?" Jake asked.

"You want to pray silently or out loud?" Claire inquired.

"Silent is fine," Jake replied, following her lead and bowing his head.

Claire pulled a jar of puréed beef baby food along with a jar of peas from the bag, opened them, and spooned half of each jar into the mashed potatoes and gravy. With the care of a chef preparing a soufflé, she carefully folded the mixture until it met her exacting specifications. While she lifted a spoonful to Michelle's mouth, Jake watched as the child opened her mouth and accepted the conglomeration as if it were some exotic delicacy. Back and forth it went: a bite of potatoes for Michelle, a bite of fruit for Claire; a drink of milk for Michelle, a drink of coffee for Claire; a bite of strained apricots for Michelle, and a bite of banana-nut bread for Claire.

"Whoops, think she's done," Claire advised when Michelle gagged slightly and shook her head. "How's your dinner?" she asked, noting that Jake had just about completed his meal.

"Pretty good. I was sure. . ."

Before he could finish his sentence, Michelle gave a loud burp, gagged, and proceeded to vomit her entire meal. Claire jumped from her chair and grabbed a small towel from the backpack, Jake searched for additional napkins, and the surrounding customers appeared stupefied by the event.

"You want to get us some towels from the kitchen?" Jake asked, grabbing the arm of a passing waitress who hadn't witnessed the event. Viewing the predicament, she scurried off and returned with a pile of white towels, deposited them on the table, and left as quickly as she'd appeared.

Calmly moving to the other side of the wheelchair, Jake began to wipe Michelle's shoes while handing Claire a few additional towels. Without comment, he worked alongside her until Michelle, the wheelchair, and surrounding area were passably clean.

"Let's get out of here," Claire whispered to Jake as she surveyed the room of astonished customers.

"If that's what you want to do. But don't leave on my account. I'm not embarrassed or uncomfortable, Claire. Won't Michelle need to eat again?" he asked.

"No, she won't be hungry after that, and I really would prefer to leave," she told him, gathering things together.

Jake flagged the waitress, grabbed the checks, and quickly paid the waitress as Claire pushed the wheelchair toward the exit. Just as she reached the door, he jumped in front of her and pulled it open.

"You're rushing around like there's a fire somewhere," he said as they reached the car.

"I know, but scenes like that are unnerving when I'm surrounded by strangers," she brusquely answered.

"I'm not a stranger, Claire. I understand she had no control over what occurred in there, and if those other people don't understand, well, I guess that's their problem. At least that's the way I see it," he said.

Turning around, she leaned back against her mahogany brown Ford and looked deep into the earnest blue eyes staring back at her. "That's another ten points for you, Jake Lindsey!"

five

Weaving among the cages in the zoo, Jake seemed to be enjoying Michelle's reactions as much as Claire. "Let's go back to the bird exhibits. She seems to like those sounds the best, don't you think?" Jake asked. Just then, one of the lions broadcast a chain of guttural sounds that culminated in one giant roar. Michelle giggled until tears rolled down her cheeks.

"I don't know, the lion seems to be getting his share of votes right now," Claire replied, laughing at Michelle's response.

After one last return to the bird cages, they left the zoo, stopped at the Dairy Queen for a strawberry sundae and, after returning Michelle home, began their trip back toward Junction City. Threading her way through traffic and back toward the interstate, Claire felt content with the day's events.

"So what happened after you and Glenn got home—you know, after visiting the pediatrician with Michelle?" Jake asked.

"Apparently you've got an excellent memory. You remember more about where I left off than I do," Claire answered, giving him a surprised look. "You sure you want more of that story?"

"I wouldn't have asked unless I wanted to hear it," he replied encouragingly.

"Like I told you, initially we were in shock. But after a period of time we had absorbed the news, and our disbelief was replaced by an undeniable 'why us' attitude. Unfortunately, as that phase wore off, we developed diametrically opposed strategies for Michelle's future. As I told you earlier, Glenn thought it would be best for all of us to institutionalize

Michelle immediately. I fought him, and he relented. However, his agreement came with the caveat that Michelle would be my responsibility, that I couldn't depend on him for the numerous doctor and hospital visits that had been forecast by the medical professionals. After that, his interaction with Michelle was minimal."

"That must have been hard on your marriage," Jake remarked.

"Both of us attempted to keep our marriage intact and for the most part, we were successful. There were scars—but all marriages go through rough times. If you're fortunate, the rough times eventually strengthen the union. Anyway, I continued to look for some kind of medical help for Michelle," she continued, turning the subject back to Michelle and away from her marriage to Glenn.

"I take it, from the way you said that, your search wasn't tremendously successful," he interjected.

"That's putting it mildly. I traveled all over the country grasping at straws, knowing there just had to be someone or something to help our daughter. I wasn't looking for a magic pill, just a way to give her a better quality of life," she explained.

"You mean you weren't expecting a miracle?" Jake inquired, watching her closely as she answered.

"I have *always* prayed for God's will in Michelle's life—and my own. If there's a miracle intended in her life, it will happen, and God will be glorified. I've never to prayed for God to make her 'normal,' although I have prayed for healing when she's been physically ill. To some people I suppose that's a cop-out, but I believe there is a purpose in every life and I have always believed Michelle would serve God in her own special way. Does that make any sense to you?" she asked.

"I guess, but I'm certainly no authority on miracles—or God's will, for that matter," Jake replied. "So did you ever find anyone willing to try and help you?"

"Oh, I can't even begin to count the number of people who

have helped us on this journey," she replied, giving him a smile. "But I think you're asking if any doctors gave me an answer, right?"

"Right," he replied, nodding.

"Along with Michelle's other problems, she had an under-developed respiratory system and suffered from several episodes of pneumonia when she was younger. She would have to be hospitalized on those occasions, and during her last hospitalization for pneumonia when she was eighteen months old, I met a registered nurse at the Junction City hospital. Because she had a daughter with similar problems, she'd been researching different avenues for assistance. Anyway, she had recently taken her daughter to Philadelphia to be evaluated for a somewhat unorthodox new program, and they had been accepted. She gave me all the literature and explained the program, telling me she was quitting work the next week in order to begin 'patterning' her daughter, LeeAnn.

"She did caution me that the program wasn't yet approved by the AMA—not because it posed any danger to the patients, rather because they weren't sure it was of any great benefit. I explained to her that AMA approval wasn't necessary to peak my interest, and I would be visiting with my doctor regarding the necessary referral. But that's when she revealed to me that obtaining a referral would be difficult. Because of the AMA's stand, most physicians weren't willing to make referrals."

"I'm sure that didn't stop you," Jake said, giving her an encouraging grin.

"Not really. I found a local doctor who was the parent of a retarded child. He reviewed the materials and said that although he didn't think the program would help, it certainly wouldn't hurt Michelle. He also added that it probably would do a great deal for me psychologically, because I would actually be *doing* something. He told me that from a parent's perspective rather than as a physician, and I've always been grateful to him.

"This is such a long story, Jake. Wouldn't you like to change the subject for a while?" she asked.

"Only if you're uncomfortable talking about it further," he responded.

"I'm not uncomfortable. I just feel as though I'm monopolizing the conversation with details that can't be all that interesting to you," she replied.

"Anything you say interests me," he answered, his voice filled with warmth.

"I doubt that!" Claire strenuously rebutted as she met his eyes. Surprised at the powerful emotion she saw in his look, Claire quickly returned her eyes to the highway.

"Are you going to continue?" Jake finally asked when Claire remained silent for several minutes.

"What? Oh, yes. Well, after receiving the referral, I approached Glenn, who was completely opposed to the whole concept. Finally, after several months he agreed. But once again, his agreement came with a caveat. I had to agree that if this program wasn't successful, Michelle would be institutionalized, which is where Glenn felt she would receive the best care," she told him.

"What did he consider 'success'?" Jake asked.

"If she hadn't shown any progress within a year of beginning the program, or if her progress stabilized for a year. Since Michelle is profoundly retarded, I thought we'd be able to see enough progress each year to keep going. Don't ask me how I came to that conclusion—I just did. Anyway, I took Michelle to Philadelphia, where she was evaluated as a candidate for the Doman-Delacato patterning program. They had an extremely competent staff; in fact, a world-renowned neurosurgeon advised me that Michelle was microcephalic and that her brain hadn't grown at a normal rate during pregnancy. Even though the doctor expressed concern that Michelle was not a top-notch candidate, I assured him I still wanted to try and would give it a one-hundred percent effort."

"So what did this program entail?" Jake asked, shifting in his seat to face her direction.

"We had to have volunteers come to the house and assist with patterning Michelle. It's a form of physical therapy that requires three people moving her body in a crawling fashion, one person at her head and one on each side of her body. The concept is an attempt to pattern the brain cells into those first necessary movements of crawling, then creeping, and ultimately walking. In addition to the patterning sessions, there were innumerable other methods of stimulation that had to be performed on a daily basis. The regimen scheduled for Michelle consisted of a daily program that began at seven in the morning and ended at six in the evening—seven days a week—no holidays. We had over one hundred volunteers who were in our house on a weekly basis, helping to perform various portions of the agenda," she told him, glancing toward him as she came to a stop at the interstate exit ramp.

"That sounds like an unbearable lifestyle. How did you ever survive it?" Jake asked, astonishment evident in his voice.

"It wasn't easy, but somehow we did."

"Where did you find the volunteers?" Jake asked.

"Oh, the radio station and newspapers were wonderful. They interviewed me on radio talk shows and encouraged folks to volunteer. Both the weekly and daily newspapers did large features explaining the process, and those stories resulted in many folks volunteering. It was a real blessing. The volunteers came to an orientation session before we began the program—just so I could explain things, give them some basic instructions, and introduce them to Michelle. I know it's hard to believe, but many of them had never seen a retarded child before. Months later, some of them confessed that they had been frightened, explaining their sense of relief when they saw that Michelle was a sweet little girl who enjoyed their devoted attention. I can't begin to relate the wonderful experiences that came out of those years of patterning.

"Looks like I've talked you all the way home," Claire told him as she stopped the car in front of the closed garage doors.

"Want to pull it in the garage?" Jake asked, unfastening his seat belt and opening the car door.

"I'll leave it here for now. I need to pick up some things at the grocery store later. I can put it away when I return. Thanks for going along—and for being such a good listener," Claire said, extending her hand.

Instead of shaking her hand, he quickly leaned down and gave her an unexpected kiss on the cheek.

"You're quite a lady," he said, turning on his heel and walking toward his car before she could object to his behavior.

"I'll give you a call next week. We'll get together so that I can hear the rest of the story," he called, waving his arm out the window as he pulled the sleek black sports car away from the curb.

≈≈

"So how did your date go?" Gloria asked from the other end of the telephone line.

"It wasn't a date, Gloria," Claire explained, a note of exasperation evident in her voice.

"Call it whatever you want. How did it go?"

"Fine. We went to the restaurant and had dinner; Michelle promptly regurgitated her entire meal; we cleaned it up, left the restaurant, went to the zoo, stopped at Dairy Queen, and came home," Claire recounted without any inflection in her voice.

"Oh, no. You mean our little Miss Michelle let him have it on his first visit?" Gloria asked, bursting out in a hearty laugh. "I know I shouldn't laugh, but I can just picture Jake. I'll bet he was ready to cut and run."

Throughout their friendship, Gloria had accompanied Claire to visit Michelle on many occasions and had observed several of Michelle's episodes of projectile vomiting.

"Believe it or not, he didn't get the least bit unnerved by the incident. In fact, he probably handled it better than I did. You know, it still bothers me when there's some kind of scene when I have Michelle out in public. Well—it sure didn't bother Jake. He even said it was obvious that Michelle had no control over what occurred in the restaurant and if the other customers didn't understand, that was their problem," Claire related.

"Good for him! So how many points did he get?" Gloria inquired, referring to Claire's habit of giving people "points" for exceptional behavior.

"Twenty," Claire promptly responded. "But don't get excited. He's a nice guy, but that doesn't mean I'm interested in him—at least not in a romantic sense," Claire clarified.

"So, in what sense *are* you interested?" Gloria shot back.

"He seems really nice—I wouldn't mind having him as a friend. And that's all I mean, Gloria. A friend, just like you, nothing more."

"I hear you. A friend is a good beginning."

"It's the beginning and the end. What are you doing this evening?" Claire asked, deliberately changing the subject.

"I'm fixing dinner for Roger, and then we're going out to Fort Riley. The new commanding general's wife has decided there's a need for a Youth Center on post. She's convinced the Officers' Wives Club to promote some fund-raisers. The first one is tonight—a fashion show," Gloria told her.

"Roger *wants* to attend a fashion show?" Claire asked in a voice filled with amazement.

"Roger *has* to attend the fashion show. He's in it!"

"You're kidding—how did that happen?" Claire inquired.

"The clothing that's being modeled is being furnished by local merchants in exchange for the promotional advertising they receive. Well, Roger generally buys his civilian clothes at Duffy's, and they suggested his name to one of the officers' wives who solicited Duffy's participation in the event. Need I say more?"

"So the officer's wife told her husband, who told Roger's

commanding officer, who passed the word along to Roger that he'd better be present, right?"

"You got it," Gloria responded. "Roger's threatening to boycott Duffy's. However, I think the owner probably thought he was paying him a compliment by suggesting him as a model. Of course, Roger isn't looking at it from the same perspective."

"So what does he have to model?" Claire inquired, never ceasing to be amazed at the military's ability to coerce its personnel into such far-fetched schemes.

"A suit and a pair of casual slacks and sweater. I think if his commanding officer would have just asked him, instead of making it an order, Roger wouldn't have minded quite so much," Gloria explained.

"Guess we're all kind of like that. I'd sure rather be asked than ordered," Claire agreed.

"Well, guess I better get out of here and get busy with dinner. I'm glad that Jake didn't turn out to be a jerk. Give me a call after you get home from church tomorrow," Gloria instructed, aware that her friend's Sunday morning schedule always included church.

"Okay. Have a good time this evening," Claire said and hung up the receiver.

Through the years, the two women had grown to respect each other's faith. Claire prayed for Gloria, and she knew Gloria did the same for her. Long ago they had agreed to disagree over religion, and it was a topic they no longer discussed. After concurring with Gloria that the subject would be off limits, Claire feared that she had made the wrong decision. However, those fears had been put to rest when, only a few weeks later, Claire listened to a sermon that dealt with the subject of witnessing through example rather than verbal sparring. That message had affirmed their decision and safeguarded an abiding friendship.

Claire completed two small loads of laundry, and when she had finished folding the last of the clothes, she freshened up and, after locking the house, left for the grocery store. It didn't take long to purchase the few items she needed, so by nine o'clock she was home, had showered, and was reading a book that would soon become overdue at the library.

Deciding to fix a glass of iced tea, she walked past the telephone on her way to the kitchen but then retraced her steps. *Maybe I ought to give Jake a call and thank him again for being so kind,* she thought, picking up the telephone and dialing the number he had left on her kitchen table the night they met.

The phone rang at the other end of the line, and Claire settled back in the antique oak rocking chair beside the small table where the telephone rested. After ten rings, she hung up. *Wonder where he is,* she thought, as she padded back to the kitchen and fixed the glass of iced tea. Settling on the couch to read, she found her thoughts occasionally drifting back to the events that had occurred earlier in the day, pleased that Jake had accompanied her.

By eleven o'clock it was obvious Claire wasn't going to finish the book that evening. Placing the bookmark inside, she found herself once again dialing Jake's phone number. It rang—but still there was no answer.

As she pulled the freshly laundered sheet under her chin, she found herself intrigued, wondering where he might be— and with whom.

six

Monday morning arrived, and Claire was greeted by the announcement that one of Lyle's cases had been moved up on the court docket. Although it hadn't been scheduled for trial until the first week of the following month, the other cases scheduled for trial had been settled.

"Tell me there's at least a possibility we're looking at a settlement," Claire said to Lyle Johnstone who, at thirty-six, was the younger of the two attorneys in the firm.

"Absolutely none," he said. "Sorry, Claire. I know you're not ready for another trial so soon, but I'm really going to need a hundred percent effort from everyone on this. Dave's agreed to allow you and Gloria to work exclusively on this trial. Josie will do any secretarial work he has, and, fortunately, he doesn't have anything else looming on the horizon—at least no other major trials," he quickly qualified.

"How much time do we have?" Claire asked.

"We're next in line. As soon as the case now being heard is complete, we're up," he told her just as Gloria was walking in the front door.

"Tell me I didn't hear what I thought I just heard," she said, leveling a grim look toward Lyle.

"I can *tell* you anything you want, but the fact is we've got to get ready for trial. I called and left word for Carl Simpson. He's defendant's counsel in the case we'll be following. I thought he could give me some idea if his case would be going to the jury in the next couple days or if there's any possibility we might have until next Monday," he told them.

"Can't you file a motion for an extension?" Claire asked hopefully.

"You know better than that, Claire. The docket clearly says. . ."

"I know, I know," she interrupted. "Be prepared for trial, no extensions granted. But maybe the judge would be a little accommodating since there were so many cases that settled. Who would have ever thought we'd be next in line?" she persuasively argued.

"Did you see which judge is assigned?" Lyle asked.

"Please tell me it's not Hackley," Gloria groaned.

"I wish I could, but unfortunately it *is* Hackley. There's no way I'm asking him for an extension. Not only would he tell me 'no' to the extension, but he'd also take every opportunity to rule against me on issues during the trial. No way I'm doing that to my client."

"You know, Lyle, it would help if this case were at least a little bit interesting," Gloria remarked as she began pulling the red expandable folders from the lateral file cabinet behind her desk.

"It *is* an interesting case. Especially to my client," Lyle retorted defensively.

"Come on you guys. Let's quit hassling about whether the case is interesting and start getting organized," Claire counseled, with a note of resignation in her voice.

"How can he think land condemnation is interesting?" Gloria whispered to Claire as the two of them began pulling depositions and making a list of witnesses that needed to be subpoenaed.

"I'm sure it is interesting to Lyle. I know he feels a lot of empathy for the people he's representing. After all, some of these folks have owned this land for generations," Claire replied.

"I know, I know, but just think how great it will be for the whole area to have a dam. Putting aside the fact that it will take care of flood control, just think about all the recreational possibilities," she continued, her eyes sparkling.

"Are you already seeing yourself out there on the water in a brand new ski boat?"

"You never know. It could happen," she replied with a laugh.

The remainder of the day passed rapidly, the two women working at a feverish pace while Lyle issued orders and then retreated to his office to dictate pretrial motions.

"I need you to go over the juror questionnaires by morning, Claire," Lyle said, as he once again emerged from the refuge of his office.

"Lyle, it's already six o'clock. I haven't taken so much as a lunch or coffee break all day," Claire replied. "Did you ever hear from Carl?" she asked, hoping for some positive information.

"Yeah. He called about five-thirty. Said they'd probably get to closing arguments tomorrow unless the plaintiff calls quite a few rebuttal witnesses. He didn't think there was any possibility they'd settle. Our only hope will be an indecisive jury," he told her, obviously attempting to remain calm.

"Well, thanks for that cheerful note. Tell you what, I'll take the questionnaires home and look them over. I can at least get you a preliminary workup on prospective jurors by morning," she said, seeing the beginning signs of panic etched on his face.

❧

"You sleep here last night?" Gloria asked Claire as she entered the law office at seven the next morning.

"Not hardly. I got here about six because I promised Lyle I'd have a preliminary workup on the jurors for him. This way I have time to get it typed before he gets here."

"How late did you stay up working on that?" Gloria asked.

"I got done about two," Claire replied, continuing to key the information.

"So you've had about three hours of sleep. You ought to be in great shape by noon," Gloria chastised her friend.

"These guys are gonna kill us with these trials. I think they need to hire some more help if they're going to keep going at this pace," she continued.

"You may be right, but we don't have time to argue the finer points of employee-employer relations right now. I suggest that you get to work on that pile of motions Lyle left on your desk. We'll talk about organizing a union after the trial," Claire joked, flashing her friend a quick smile.

"You heard any more from Jake?" Gloria asked as she positioned herself at the metal secretarial desk.

"No, I haven't. Why do you ask?"

"Just wondered. Roger called last night and said Jake was going on and on at work yesterday—telling him about what a good time you guys had on Saturday. I figured he'd probably called you, that's all," Gloria remarked.

Surprised at the sense of pleasure she felt upon hearing the comment, Claire felt a blush rise in her cheeks. She hoped Gloria wasn't watching.

"What kind of progress are we making?" Lyle asked as he appeared in the office at nine o'clock.

"We wouldn't be making any if we *all* waited until nine o'clock to come to work," Gloria impulsively replied.

"You know, Gloria, if you weren't such a good legal secretary, I wouldn't put up with your audacity," he bantered.

"Ah, come on, Lyle, you wouldn't know how to act if I treated you any other way," she replied.

They all three laughed, easing the mounting tension that invariably crept into their lives whenever there were long hours of trial preparation looming ahead. Perhaps to an outsider, Gloria's undaunted cheekiness would probably have appeared insubordinate. But they were a small office, and instead of offending the bosses, she generally got a laugh out of them. Claire admired her friend's innate ability to know when to keep her mouth shut and when to toss out a quick repartee. If nothing else, Gloria had excellent timing.

Claire's strengths within the office were more tangible. She didn't want to use her time running for coffee and sandwiches, easing rising tensions, or patting people on the back for performing their jobs. Instead, she wanted to produce, organize, and, above all, be prepared for any circumstance that might occur in trial. Dave and Lyle had often been pleasantly surprised when an event developed during trial and Claire could produce the document or research papers they needed to move forward immediately with an argument. Both attorneys had encouraged her to go back to school and get her law degree, promising her a partnership after she completed the grueling hours of academia. She promptly refused.

Claire was rather private regarding her personal life. Dave and Lyle assumed that Glenn had left her huge insurance policies and retirement funds. They thought she worked more in an effort to fill her time than to earn money. Not that they actually said those words. It was more in the comments they occasionally made about their rich, widowed legal assistant, along with the fact that when they gave raises or Christmas bonuses, they would remark that the money probably wouldn't mean much to her. But Glenn *hadn't* left large insurance policies or investments.

Shortly after his death when Claire had called several insurance companies in order to apply for payment, she found that Glenn had borrowed on the policies, never paying back the loans. She had been shocked to learn that the value on all of them had diminished to almost nothing. He did have one policy through his employer that was a straight life policy with no loan value. Fortunately, it had been enough to pay for the hospital expenses not covered by their medical insurance, as well as the funeral. A check for Glenn's accrued vacation days and his final paycheck were the remainder of his "estate."

It was during those grief-filled days that Claire realized how little she knew about their finances. All of Michelle's medical bills, the cost of flying back and forth across the country, staying in hotels, seeking out and using medical professionals, purchasing special wheelchairs and equipment, were all neatly combined in two large folders. Little had been covered by their medical insurance, but Glenn never told her of the struggle to pay the mounting debts. It appeared that he had first depleted all of their savings and certificates of deposit; next he cashed the bonds they had begun purchasing for Michelle when she was born; then he withdrew his retirement funds; finally, he borrowed against his life insurance policies.

For months after his death, Claire had been in a daze, angry at herself for paying no attention to the finances, never questioning how the bills were being paid. Deep in her heart she hadn't wanted to know, afraid that if she inquired, Glenn would have yet another reason for institutionalizing Michelle. And she didn't want to hear those words.

After days of sorting through all of the papers, paying the outstanding bills, and doing a final tally, there was no doubt that she must continue to work. Without Glenn's income, she would be fortunate to keep her head above water. The one thing Glenn hadn't mortgaged was their home, and Claire was immeasurably thankful that he had stopped short of that act. She wasn't sure why he hadn't taken that ultimate step. Perhaps because Claire would have been required to sign the mortgage papers, or perhaps because it had been the family home he grew up in, willed to him by his parents at their death. In retrospect, Claire occasionally wondered how many important papers she had signed, never questioning what they were as he shoved them before her and offered a pen. She probably would have unwittingly signed mortgage papers on the house had Glenn asked for her signature—she was thankful he hadn't.

"I'm going down to the Good Eats and grab some lunch. Want to come along?" Gloria asked as she pulled her purse from the bottom desk drawer.

"I'd better stay and get this done," Claire replied, nodding toward the sheaf of paperwork on her desk.

"It'll be there when we get back. You need to take a break, Claire. You've been here since six this morning. Come on," Gloria urged.

"Yeah, go with her," Lyle chimed in as he walked into the conference room where the two women had been working. "It'll do you good to get out of here for a while. Besides, you can bring me something to eat," he quickly added.

"You work too hard, Claire," Gloria admonished as the two of them walked toward the small cafe down the street. "You know the old saying, 'all work and no play'," her friend chanted.

"Yeah, yeah. If this lunch break is going to be spent listening to you lecture me, I'll go back to work," Claire warned affably.

"Hey, look who's here!" Gloria exclaimed in mock surprise.

Claire turned to see Roger and Jake walking through the front door of the cafe. Both were out of uniform, appearing to be off work for the day. She felt a warmth as her eyes met Jake's, a sense of genuine pleasure to see him. *Hold it! You'd better watch yourself,* she thought, sending an immediate warning to her brain.

Gloria waved, and the two men walked toward the booth. "You invited them, didn't you?" Claire whispered across the gray Formica tabletop.

"Of course," Gloria responded, keeping her eyes on Roger.

"Why didn't you tell me?" Claire quizzed, her voice becoming louder.

"Probably because she figured you wouldn't join us," Jake replied, sliding into the booth beside her. "Hi," he added and, in one fluid motion, leaned down and kissed her on the cheek.

"Hi—and don't do that," Claire replied in an ominous tone.

"I guess you've been warned," Roger said, shaking his finger at Jake.

"Sorry," Jake told Claire. "I was just glad to see you. No offense intended. You sure look nice," he continued, surveying her appearance.

"You both take the day off, or have they changed military attire from fatigues to blue jeans?" Claire inquired while Roger and Gloria slipped into deep conversation.

"It's military payday," Jake responded.

"Oh, I forgot. You Army types get off at noon on paydays. That's a nice little perk," Claire replied, with a note of envy in her voice.

"You, too, can have all of the Army's perks, Claire. All you've gotta do is see your local recruiter," he responded, not allowing her comment to ruffle him.

"Two points for you," she said, looking down at the menu, realizing her comment had been uncalled for.

"Let's see, I think that gives me twenty-two of those famous points. What do I get when I reach a hundred?" he asked, giving her an engaging smile.

"I don't give prizes—just points," she responded.

"You ought to think about it."

"Think about what?" she asked.

"Giving prizes—you know—the old Pavlov theory. When you perform properly, you get a treat. Points aren't much of a treat. You need to have at least some kind of reward for reaching a goal of every twenty-five points or so," he explained while retaining a serious countenance.

"You're joking, right?" Claire asked, giving him a small grin.

"Not if I can talk you into my theory," he said. "How about something like at twenty-five points I get to go see Michelle again, at fifty points I get to kiss you, at seventy-five points, we date each other exclusively. . ."

"I don't think so," Claire interrupted, not wanting to hear the reward for one hundred points.

"I don't know why not. *You* control the points," he

responded, giving her a wink. "What are you going to have?" he asked, changing the subject.

"The club sandwich," she replied.

"How's Michelle?" he asked.

"Fine."

"You going over to see her this weekend?"

"I don't know. We're preparing for another trial. Depends on what I can get squeezed in," she responded honestly.

"I tried to call you last night to see if I could go with you the next time you go see her. Didn't get any answer," he said.

"I had to work late. I'll probably be working late all week. If I get to go it will be on the spur of the moment. I really can't make definite plans when we're preparing for trial," Claire explained.

"You could give me a call. I can be ready pretty quickly," he argued doggedly.

"As a matter of fact, I tried to call you Saturday night. I didn't get an answer," she countered.

"Let's see, Saturday night. Oh, I remember. After leaving you on Saturday I went home for a while, and then some of the guys got together to play some basketball over at King Field House," he explained.

"I didn't know the gym stayed open that late," she remarked.

He didn't respond to her comment.

seven

At the last minute, they lucked out. Carl Simpson's jury had deadlocked, with the judge declaring a mistrial on Thursday afternoon. To Lyle's relief, the court clerk had called advising that Judge Hackley didn't want to begin impaneling a jury until Monday.

"That's a comfort," Claire sighed, as soon as Lyle related the news.

"How many hours can you give me this weekend?" Lyle immediately inquired of the two women.

"Aw, come on, Lyle," Gloria pleaded. "We've got the rest of today and all day tomorrow. Can't you finish up before the weekend?"

Glancing at Claire, he gave her a hopeful look. "What about you, Claire? Can you give me any time over the weekend?" he inquired.

"I can work late Friday night, and I can give you some time on Saturday. Sunday's out. I'm going to church in the morning and want to go see Michelle in the afternoon," she explained.

"It's a deal," he quickly agreed. "I'll have my dictation completed so that you don't have to work on Saturday if you can work late Friday," he said, quickly turning his attention toward Gloria. "Can you live with that?" he asked.

"I guess," she replied mournfully. "As long as I get out of here by ten o'clock. I want to spend at least a couple hours with Roger," she told Lyle.

"I promise," he said, obviously delighted with the bargains he'd struck with each of them.

"You seeing Jake this weekend?" Gloria asked when Lyle had gone back to his office.

"I don't think so," Claire answered.

"How come? Bet he'd be more than willing to go with you Sunday afternoon."

"Maybe. We'll see," she absently replied, not wanting to say anything that Gloria might repeat to Roger. It was part of the way Gloria operated when she was in her matchmaking mode. Anything that might be fodder toward building their relationship would be passed along to Roger and then forwarded to Jake.

The remainder of Thursday and all day Friday passed in a frenzy of activity. Claire scheduled their witnesses to come in for last-minute briefings on Saturday. Lyle had split the list between the two of them. He was interviewing the witnesses that were more difficult to control. She had just walked into the reception area to get Marian Roseman when Jake walked into the office.

"What are you doing here?" she asked, walking toward him and impeding his further entrance into the waiting room.

"I wanted to see if you could go out this evening," he answered loudly enough to gain Mrs. Roseman's attention.

"You can go into my office, Mrs. Roseman. I'll be with you in a few minutes," Claire instructed the woman.

The two of them watched silently as the woman carefully folded the newspaper she'd been reading, placed it in a rack, and then slowly ambled toward Claire's office.

"I'd rather not discuss my personal life in front of clients," Claire admonished Jake as soon as the woman was out of earshot.

"Sorry. I didn't realize the possibility of going somewhere with me this evening should be a secret," he whispered, making her feel foolish for reproving him.

"It's not that going somewhere with you is a secret. It's just that I'm a rather private person. I don't like everyone knowing my personal business," she said in an attempt to make her remark seem logical.

"I'll take that statement to mean we're going out. Where would you like to go?" he asked, giving her a grin.

"I think you must have heard something I didn't say," she responded, returning his smile. "Honestly, Jake, I'm just too tired to go anywhere this evening, but thanks for asking. I've really got to get in there," she said, pointing toward her office.

"How about tomorrow?" he persisted. "Can we go see Michelle?"

"I'll give you a call if I think we can work it out," she responded.

"Now there's an answer that doesn't tell me a thing. What does that mean? If *you* think *we* can work it out?" he asked. "Why don't you just give me a call and *we'll* see if *we* can work it out."

"Okay, okay. Now I've really got to get in there," she told him, opening the front door in an attempt to hurry him along.

"I can take a hint—don't forget to call me," he said, once again swooping down and placing a kiss on her cheek.

Before Claire could say a word, he walked out the door. "I know, I know—*don't do that*," he called back over his shoulder, waving his arm in the air, the familiar car keys dangling from his hand.

The meeting with Mrs. Roseman had taken much longer than Claire anticipated. After an hour of talking with the woman, Claire was sure that Mrs. Roseman should have been on Lyle's list.

"I just don't understand how this can be happening," the older woman once again insisted. "If my Donald were alive, he would have stopped this. You people would have never taken our land," she avowed, her voice wavering, obviously close to tears.

"Mrs. Roseman, if you will listen very closely, I'm going to try and explain this once again. First of all, Mr. Johnstone is the attorney representing you; he is not attempting to take your land. It's the Corps of Engineers that has filed the land condemnation action against all of the residents of Lyndon," Claire began.

"The Corps of Engineers? John Ingmire said it was the government that was taking our land," the woman immediately interrupted.

"The Corps of Engineers is a branch of the government, Mrs. Roseman. Because of the flooding that has occurred in this part of the state, the Corps of Engineers—or government, if you prefer—has decided that a dam needs to be built to control the possibility of flooding in the future. After several years of studies, they have concluded that the best possible site for the dam is along a line just to the east of Lyndon. This means that the whole community will be underwater once the dam is completed. In order to move forward with this project, it's necessary for the corps—government—to condemn and purchase the property of you folks who were unwilling to make outright sales to them."

"Well, why should I sell it to them? I don't want to move! My family has lived on that farm for generations," she argued.

"I'm not saying you should have agreed. I'm simply explaining how the process works," Claire patiently continued. "What we are attempting to do through our lawsuit is have the government look at a different site to build the dam. One where no one will be dislocated."

"See, now, that makes sense," the woman agreed. "That's probably why John Ingmire told me I should be in on this thing," she said, obviously referring to the lawsuit.

"Probably," Claire agreed, trying to keep from becoming exasperated. "You must understand that this lawsuit is twofold, Mrs. Roseman. If the jury finds that the government is correct and that Lyndon is the best site, their next step will be to decide if the prices the government has offered for your land are fair."

"You mean the jury gets to say how much money I should have?" she inquired.

"Could you wait here just a few minutes? I need to visit with Mr. Johnstone for a moment," Claire requested and promptly went to Josie's desk. Dialing the intercom number for Lyle's office, she let it ring until he finally picked up the phone.

"Yes!" he snapped.

"I'm sorry to bother you, Lyle, but I really need to talk to you. Can you come out here for a few minutes," Claire requested.

"Can't it wait?" he asked.

"No, we've got a problem with Mrs. Roseman. I think maybe she's senile."

"I'll be right there," he replied, slamming down the phone.

"I don't think I want to hear this," Lyle said, walking into the front office where Claire stood waiting.

"Honestly, Lyle, it's as if she doesn't have any idea why she's joined in this lawsuit except that John Ingmire told her it was a good idea. I've explained the whole process three times, and she still doesn't understand. I even checked to make sure she attended the original meeting where the plaintiffs voted to file suit. She signed the attendance sheet. Not only that, she's attended every meeting since then. Her name's on all the attendance sheets, and I even performed a cursory check to see if it looked like someone else had been signing her name. It doesn't. Do you want me to call one of her neighbors or see if she has a relative I can talk to?"

"Guess you'd better. Tell her she can go home and we'll talk to her later. Be sure to explain that she doesn't need to attend the trial. I won't call her as a witness, and I sure don't want to take a chance that she'll show up in court and cause any problems," he instructed.

Claire watched as Lyle strode toward his office and then went back to where Mrs. Roseman patiently sat waiting.

"I think that's all we need to go over today, Mrs. Roseman," Claire told the woman. "By the way, do you have any children who live nearby?"

"Never was able to have children," she calmly explained.

"Closest thing to a living relative I got is Donald's niece, Phyllis."

"Where does Phyllis live?" Claire asked.

"I'm not really sure, now that you ask. I haven't had a Christmas card from her for several years—probably not since Donald passed."

"Do you know her last name?' Claire ventured, not wanting to sound insulting but hoping she could gain some additional information.

"Mueller, Mohler, I don't know—something like that. Doesn't really matter. I never was close to her—just exchanged Christmas cards. Why do you ask?"

"Oh, I was just wondering who you counted on for help when you need it," Claire replied.

"God, of course," the woman quickly replied, causing Claire to give her a warm smile in return.

"Of course. But I was wondering if there was any *person* who helped you out from time to time," Claire questioned further.

"Oh, sometimes John—John Ingmire. He lives close by, and if he's feeling good enough, he'll lend a hand. Marty Watson's boy shovels my snow and mows the grass in summer. Is that what you're talking about?" the woman asked.

"Sure, that's fine. Incidentally, do you have a doctor you go to in Lyndon, or do you come over here to Junction City?" Claire attempted.

"Dr. Bogan over here in Junction. If you're looking for a doctor, he's a good one."

"I'll keep that in mind," Claire replied. "I guess we're through. I'll call you if we need to discuss anything else. Just remember, there's no need for you to attend the trial," Claire emphasized.

"Right! Unless John tells me I should," she replied. "Could you call me a taxi, dear? I'll just wait out front where I can watch until it arrives."

"I'd be happy to," Claire replied, picking up the phone and dialing the Yellow Cab Company.

As soon as the taxi arrived and Mrs. Roseman was safely on her way, Claire placed her notes on the table outside Lyle's office. It was too late to call Dr. Bogan and check on the woman's medical condition, and Lyle could instruct John Ingmire to encourage Mrs. Roseman to remain at home throughout the trial. She wasn't going to interrupt Lyle to tell him she was leaving. He might convince her to stay a little longer, and she was exhausted.

By the time she left the office, it was almost eight o'clock. Her stomach was growling, and the beckoning neon sign at the Good Eats cafe caught her attention. *Think I'll just grab a bite to eat so that I don't have to bother fixing anything at home,* she thought as she walked on down the street toward the restaurant.

She seated herself in one of the smaller wooden booths and grabbed the menu that was resting behind the metal napkin holder.

"You alone tonight?" the waitress inquired, holding two glasses of water and two sets of silverware.

"Yes," Claire replied.

"I never guess it right," the girl remarked, glancing at the extra utensils and water.

Claire grinned. "Guess I'll have the special. Is there a newspaper I could read while I'm waiting?"

"Sure. I'll bring it right back," the girl replied.

Claire was glad she had stopped. With the exception of a few customers who came in and sat at the counter, the restaurant had been quiet. She'd read through the paper, received permission to work the crossword puzzle, although she'd not been overly successful, and felt much better by the time she walked out the door. It was close to nine o'clock, but the town was relatively quiet. The Saturday night drinking crowd was just beginning to make an appearance on the streets.

Pulling up to a stop light at Washington and Ash Streets, Claire sat watching as people parked their cars and walked toward the entrance of the Odyssey Club, a local favorite by all accounts. Just as the light turned green and Claire began to pull forward, she thought she caught a glimpse of Jake entering the club.

It couldn't have been Jake, she thought, turning the corner and beginning to circle the block. *What are you doing?* a small voice inside her asked.

Stopping the car, she made a U-turn and headed toward home. "He's nothing to me. Why should I be checking to see if it's him?" she murmured.

The telephone was ringing as she walked in the back door. Tossing her purse and a briefcase full of papers on the kitchen table, she grabbed the receiver.

"Hello," she answered.

"Every time I call it sounds as though you've been jogging," came the voice at the other end of the line.

"Hi, Jake. What are you up to?" she inquired. *Obviously it wasn't him I saw*, she thought to herself.

"Nothing much, just talking to you. So what time are we leaving tomorrow?" he asked.

"I didn't know *we* had made a decision that *we* were going," she responded, giving him a dose of his own medicine.

"How about it? I promise I'll be on my best behavior," he joked.

"Do you feel up to a Disney movie? Michelle loves animated films and I noticed in today's newspaper they're screening *Snow White* again. However, I certainly understand if it's not your idea of an exciting afternoon," she continued.

"Sounds great. Nothing better than a movie filled with poisoned apples and a bunch of short little guys," he said, giving her a laugh. "What time do you want to leave?"

"The movie starts at two. If we leave at one, that should give us plenty of time to pick up Michelle and get there. We won't go out to eat this time," she said, a lilt in her voice.

"Hey, I can handle it, if you can," he egged her on.

"Let's just do the movie. You want me to pick you up?" she asked.

"Nah. I don't mind driving to your place and leaving my car. It's probably safer in front of your house than it is at my apartment complex. I'll be at your place by one o'clock."

"See you then," Claire responded and hung up the phone.

Before doing anything else, she once again picked up the phone and dialed Michelle's house.

"Is that you, Sandra?" Claire inquired of the voice at the other end of the line.

"Sure is, Claire. You calling to check on our little Miss Michelle?"

"Partially. I'm planning on coming over tomorrow. I thought we'd go see *Snow White*. Could you leave a note for the staff to feed her lunch and have her ready to go at one o'clock?"

"You got it," Sandra replied in a bouncy voice. "You want her to wear something special, or should I just pick out what I like?"

"How about that new pair of brown slacks with the matching shirt—you know, the one with the little sunflowers on it?" Claire suggested.

"Oh, that's a good choice. She's been doing just fine this past week—no sniffles, no asthma attacks, and no constipation," Sandra diligently reported.

"Thanks, Sandra. Give her a kiss for me," Claire said and placed the receiver back in its cradle.

❧

"I should have asked Jake if he wanted to go to church," Claire said aloud as she walked into the bedroom an hour later. *Wonder if it's too late to call him*, she mused. Glancing at the small alarm clock beside her table, she decided he'd probably still be awake. After all, it was only eleven o'clock.

Pulling the piece of paper containing his phone number from her wallet, she walked to the living room, picked up the phone, and dialed. The phone rang at the other end of the line. There was no answer.

eight

Jake arrived promptly at one o'clock the next afternoon, wearing a pair of navy slacks, a pale blue pullover sports shirt, and black loafers. His sunglasses were tucked in the pocket of his shirt, and he carried a small bouquet of daisies, which he offered to Claire when she opened the front door.

"They'll just wilt and die in a trash can if you don't take them," he said.

"I'm not sure. . ."

"They're just flowers, Claire, not a lifetime commitment," he interrupted, forcing them into her hand.

"Let me find a vase," she replied, walking into the kitchen and opening the cabinet doors underneath the sink. "Success!" she said, holding out a blue and gray pottery container.

He watched as she filled the vase with water, removed the paper wrapping, took a pair of scissors and snipped off the bottom of each stem, and then arranged the flowers, spreading them apart to fill the stoneware receptacle. Carefully, she lifted it from the counter and placed it in the center of the kitchen table.

"Thank you, Jake. Daisies are one of my favorite flowers," she said, gracing him with a smile.

"You're most welcome. Want me to do the driving?" he offered.

Claire hesitated for just a moment. "That would be great. Driving isn't one of my favorite things, especially when I'm tired," she admitted.

"So are you planning on sleeping through the movie?" he teased.

"Not a chance. When I take Michelle to a movie, I spend

my time watching her," Claire answered as they walked into the garage.

Pulling the pair of sunglasses from his shirt pocket, Jake flipped them open and slid the aviator-style glasses onto his face. "Now that I've got you all to myself, how about finishing your life history for me?" he asked as they moved toward the stop sign at the end of the street.

"I don't even remember where we were. Besides, I think it's time I heard about you," Claire replied.

"You finish your story on the way there, and I'll talk on the way home," he offered. "You had told me about beginning to pattern and all the volunteers," he said, refreshing her memory.

"Well, the patterning lasted six years. From the time Michelle was two until she was eight. In the first four years, we never missed a day unless Michelle was sick. When I was sick, the volunteers carried on. I had a wonderful coordinator who took care of scheduling volunteers, which was a tremendous help. Anyway, during the first four years, the doctors charted progress, although Glenn was skeptical. Michelle learned to sit up, and though she couldn't actually crawl on her own, she learned to get around by rolling on her hip. She began to get into a creeping position and rock back and forth, and sometimes she would balance on her knees in an upright position. I viewed all of it as progress while Glenn felt she would have done as well on her own and even better if professionals had been working with her.

"But he kept his word, and as long as the doctors reported there was improvement, he didn't fight her continuation in the program. During the fifth year her progress slowed considerably, and although the doctors charted some slight advances, they were minimal. At that time, Glenn asked me to quit but I objected, telling him he had agreed that we could continue until the doctors charted a full year without progress. Unfortunately, that occurred during the sixth year. That's not to say she didn't make some small headway, but the doctors agreed that it couldn't be attributed to the patterning.

"Glenn didn't lose any time. He had already checked into the available programs throughout the area, and immediately upon our return home, handed me the folder of information and told me to make a choice. After reading the brochures and researching as much as possible, I finally agreed to visit two of the institutions. Reluctantly, I agreed her name could be placed on the waiting list at the Kansas Neurological Institute. My one thread of hope was the fact that *they* had a waiting list. We were told that, barring unforeseen circumstances, it could be up to three years before they would have space available. I was overjoyed. Glenn was morose, angry with himself for overlooking that detail when he was collecting information about the various institutions."

"Well, at least one thing was going your way. So you got to spend several years just enjoying Michelle, without all the patterning and extra people in the house?" Jake inquired.

"I wish. As it turned out, that remark about *barring unforeseen circumstances* came back to haunt me. The institution received a tax windfall six months later and was able to hire additional staff as well as resume its building program. The placement administrator called Glenn and advised we could admit Michelle just seven months after we'd been there. I was devastated," Claire confessed.

"Those were some of the darkest days of my life, and I still don't talk much about it. I became extremely depressed, and had it not been for my faith in God, I don't think I would have survived. After several months, our family doctor urged me to begin seeking a job. He thought it would help if I got out of the house. During the seven months before Michelle was institutionalized, I took several night classes in the paralegal program at the local university. I had seen it advertised as a new program at the college, and Glenn agreed that it would be good for me to expand my horizons beyond the house. I'd attended college right out of high school and received my degree in political science, but then Glenn and I married and I had never worked outside the home. In retrospect, I think he realized I would need something to fill my days. Anyway, my general education classes transferred toward the paralegal program. I finally completed the requirements and received my degree. I was already working at Wilmott and Johnstone by that time and was going to school at night. It didn't leave a lot of time to think," she stated, staring at Jake's profile and liking what she saw.

He glanced her way, flashing a warm smile that stirred emotions she didn't ever want to experience again. *I've got to quit seeing him*, she resolutely declared to herself.

"Go on," he encouraged, clearly unaware of her thoughts.

"That's about it—I went to work for Dave Wilmott and Lyle Johnstone, and I'm still there," she said.

"That can't be it, Claire. Michelle isn't at the Neurological Institute, and Glenn is dead," he replied. "I'm sorry. That was callous of me," he immediately apologized before she could say anything.

"You're right; it isn't everything. About two years ago Glenn had a massive heart attack. We were attending a church retreat in Colorado, and he'd gone hiking with several of the men. From what they told me, he began to have difficulty breathing, and by the time they realized he was in distress, it was too late. Apparently they made heroic attempts to resuscitate him—at least that's what the hospital personnel told me—but it all failed. A few months after his death, I began checking on alternative care for Michelle. More and more was becoming available outside of the institutional setting, and I decided that although I couldn't afford to quit work and bring Michelle home, I wanted her in a family-oriented environment that was closer to where I lived. About a year ago, I settled on the group home where she's now located."

"And are you happy with the decision?" he asked.

"Yes," she said, giving him a smile. "I get to see her more

often, and it's much nicer to visit in her home rather than an institutional ward among all the other children."

"I'm glad it's worked out well," he said in a genuinely kind voice.

"Me too," Claire agreed just as they arrived at the group home.

Michelle was ready and waiting in the sunflower outfit Claire had requested, her dark brown hair recently shampooed and her white shoes sporting a fresh coat of polish.

"Don't you look pretty," Jake commented to Michelle as he tousled her hair.

Claire smiled at the comment, unexpectedly surprised at his relaxed countenance on only his second visit. Jake pushed the wheelchair to the car, and after Claire transferred Michelle into the automobile, he collapsed the chair and placed it in the trunk.

"We've about got that down to a science," he remarked as he sat down in the driver's seat.

"Just about," Claire replied, watching as he expertly backed the car out while making a clucking noise that caused Michelle to laugh.

"She's got the cutest giggle," he commented. "No wonder Sandra's always trying to make her laugh."

࠘

Jake carefully maneuvered the wheelchair as they entered the theater. Finding the only place to position Michelle's chair was in the back of the theater where she would be unable to view the screen, he promptly wheeled down the aisle and transferred her into one of the regular seats.

"She'll be too low in the seat to see," Claire told him.

Going back to where he had positioned the wheelchair, he popped out the removable seat of her specially built chair and carried it to where Claire and Michelle sat.

"Slip this under her," he instructed Claire as he lifted Michelle.

It worked beautifully, and although Claire noticed they were receiving some stares during the episode, it didn't seem to bother Jake in the least.

"Can't remember when I've enjoyed *Snow White* so much," he said after they had taken Michelle home.

Claire grinned.

"I mean it! I had a good time," he insisted.

"I'm glad," she said. "Okay, now it's my turn to hear about your life," she told him as they began the trip home.

"I was born in Nebraska. My mother stills lives there; my father is dead. I have three sisters who all live in Florida. I joined the Navy right after I graduated from high school. . ."

"The Navy?" she interrupted.

"Right! The Navy. I did a four-year hitch and then got out and went back to Nebraska. Worked for a bridge-building contractor for about five months and decided that was no life for me. So I enlisted in the Army."

"How come you didn't go back into the Navy?" she asked.

"The Navy was okay, but I didn't think I wanted to make a career of living on a ship. So I joined the Army and made a career of living in foxholes—hypothetically speaking at least," he said. "I've been in the Army ever since. That's about all there is."

"Wait a minute, I gave you more detail than that," she said feigning indignation.

"Well, I've already told you that I've done three tours in Vietnam, two tours in Germany, and the longest I've spent at a military base stateside is here at Fort Riley. What else can I tell you? I had the usual high school romances, and one serious relationship years ago. It didn't work out," he told her.

"So is that why you've never gotten married?"

He gave her a hearty laugh. "No, not hardly."

"Then how come?" she persisted.

"The military isn't any kind of life for married folks. Just look at the divorce rate," he stated.

"There are married couples in the military that do just fine. I don't think the divorce rate is much greater in the military than elsewhere."

"I think you're wrong, but putting that aside, it never appealed to me to make a commitment to spend my life with someone and then leave her behind at least fifty percent of the time to raise the kids and worry about whether her husband was alive. Besides, back when I was young enough that I might have considered marriage, I never met anyone I thought I couldn't live without," he said.

"Ten points for honesty, Jake," she said, and then caught herself.

"Let's see—I'm up to thirty-two points, now. I'm glad you insisted that I add more to my story," he said, giving her a wink.

"Looks like I talked you home this time," he said, walking her to the back door.

"You may have done some talking, but I'm not sure I heard as much about your life as you've heard about mine," Claire admonished as she placed her key in the door.

"Here, I'll get that for you," he said, turning the key and pushing the door open for her.

"Thanks." As she turned to tell him good night, he gathered her into his arms. Pulling her to him with an unyielding urgency, he covered her lips with a yearning, passionate kiss. She felt herself returning his ardor, her whole being succumbing to the undeniable pleasure of once again being held in the protective arms of a man.

"I know, I know—*don't do that*," he whispered as she pulled away.

She nodded her head, walked inside the door, and watched as he waved his arm in the familiar manner—his car keys dangling from his hand.

nine

On Monday morning, the trial began in earnest. Claire placed a call to Dr. Bogan's office and explained the situation to his nurse. After receiving the nurse's assurance that she would call back during the noon recess, Claire joined Lyle in the courtroom just as the judge was ruling on the last of the pretrial motions.

"How'd you do?" Claire inquired as she sat down beside Lyle.

"Okay. They lost on their motion to strike our expert witness. That was the only one I was really worried about. Were you able to reach Doc Bogan?"

"No, but I talked to his nurse. She's got the information and is going to consult with him and call back during noon recess," she replied as she pulled the sheaf of paperwork dealing with the prospective jurors from a thick folder.

The morning plodded along slowly. There had been so much publicity about the impending dam project that there were few residents who hadn't formed some type of opinion regarding the land condemnation of the Lyndon community.

"I don't mean to sound impertinent, Your Honor, but you'll recall the fact that you denied my request for a change of venue," Lyle stated when the judge requested a sidebar. It was obvious the judge was growing irritated with the attorneys' various objections and the number of jurors who had already been struck from the panel.

"I don't need to be reminded of my own rulings, Mr. Johnstone. I'm not senile," the judge retorted. "I'm telling you gentlemen that I want a jury seated *today* and this trial to begin first thing tomorrow. I suggest you quit nit-picking so that we can move forward. I don't like things to bog down in my courtroom."

"Yes, sir," both men stated. Bill Statler, lead counsel for the defense, gave Lyle a smirk as they returned to their respective chairs.

By five o'clock the jury had been selected, although neither of the attorneys seemed particularly pleased.

"Bill seems just as unhappy as you. Perhaps that's a good sign," Claire said to Lyle as they left the courthouse.

"We'll have to hope you're right," Lyle pessimistically replied. "I hope Gloria got my opening statement typed up before she left work."

"I'm sure she wouldn't leave unless it was completed, Lyle. Don't start looking for trouble," Claire admonished him.

"Did you ever talk to Bogan's nurse?"

"Yes, but she didn't call back until shortly before one-thirty, so I didn't get a chance to brief you."

"So? What'd she say?"

"Lyle, you need to take a deep breath and count to ten, or we're not going to make it through this trial. This is only the first day, and if you can't do better than this after one day of Judge Hackley, we're really in trouble," Claire replied, surprised by his demeanor. Lyle was the steady, dependable partner of the law practice. Nothing flustered him and he was always prepared.

"I'm sorry, Claire. I know I'm on edge. Just give me the scoop, will you?"

"The doctor said that Mrs. Roseman has dementia. He's tried to get her into a nursing home but has been unsuccessful. Like me, he's been unable to find any living relatives. He's not even sure that the niece she occasionally talks about really exists."

"Great! So in the midst of all of this, we've got to get a guardian appointed for her. Otherwise, if there's a settlement offer after we've presented our evidence, she won't be competent to sign the agreement."

"I can start the paperwork; Dave can handle the court appearances. With a little luck, we'll be able to get a guardian appointed without too much difficulty," Claire said, although, knowing Lyle, she figured he was already ten steps ahead of her.

If Gloria had been at the office when they returned, Claire would have cajoled her into helping with the paperwork. Unfortunately, she was gone, but Lyle wouldn't rest until he felt something was moving forward to resolve the problem with Mrs. Roseman.

The pleadings were typed and ready for filing by eleven o'clock. "I'm leaving, Lyle," Claire called from her office.

"Wait a minute. I'll walk with you—it's too late to be going out alone," he said, emerging from his office.

"I'm sorry I've acted like such a jerk today, Claire. My apologies. And thanks for staying to get those pleadings done. I really do appreciate all your hard work," he said, giving her an impulsive hug.

"Thanks, Lyle. It's okay—really," she said, surprised at his sudden show of emotion.

Claire appreciated his thoughtfulness, but on the way home she tried to remember a time when Lyle had ever shown any affection or emotion toward her. She couldn't. It seemed as if his whole personality had begun to unravel with this trial.

Lyle was an extremely brilliant attorney, having graduated Order of the Coif, the most prestigious scholastic honor given to law school graduates. He had proven himself worthy of the award. His practice reflected a dedication to detail and hard work.

Dave, on the other hand, was of average intelligence, although he, too, had built a fine reputation as an honest, hard-working lawyer. The two men were as opposite as day and night. But their differences served to enhance their joint practice. What one didn't like to do, the other enjoyed, with only a few exceptions. They had agreed early in their practice that they would not handle divorces and would accept criminal work on only a limited basis. They had held to that agreement.

Dave was married to his high school sweetheart, Peg, had three small children, resided in a sprawling house in one of the wealthier sections of town, and drove a Mercedes. In contrast, Lyle had never married, lived in an apartment in a middle-class neighborhood, and drove a dilapidated Volkswagen Beetle. He was just under six feet tall and of average build with hair resembling the color of cinnamon. Sometimes it appeared reddish-brown and other times it appeared to be more brownish-red. His eyes were a deeper shade of brown and his overall demeanor was unremarkable. It was Lyle's personality that made him appear more attractive. Although Claire now thought of him as a handsome man, when she had first met Lyle, she had considered him rather plain.

When Claire had first begun working at the office, Gloria had confided that rumor had it that Lyle had been left standing at the altar. Supposedly he had never recovered; at least not enough that he was willing to begin a relationship with another woman. At that time, the story hadn't interested Claire, but tonight she found herself wondering about Lyle and the impulsive hug. *This is silly*, she thought to herself. *Lyle Johnstone gave you a friendly hug, and you're making a federal case out of it.*

After finally arriving home and relaxing under a hot shower, Claire impulsively picked up the phone and dialed Jake's number. She didn't sit down—she didn't expect an answer. He was never at home.

"Hello," came a voice from the other end of the line, just as she was about to hang up.

"Jake?"

"Yeah, who's this?" he asked, his voice sounding different.

"It's Claire. Is something wrong? You don't sound like yourself."

"Oh, hi, Claire. No, nothing's wrong; I was just asleep.

We're going to the field tomorrow, so I've got to be out at Custer Hill by four in the morning. That means I have to leave here by three-thirty, so I turned in early. I tried to call you, but there wasn't an answer."

"I had to work late—the trial," she explained. "What does 'going to the field' entail?" she asked.

"It's another one of those special parties that Uncle Sam throws for his soldiers. We get to go out and play war games, sleep in our tents, and eat C-rations. Like most of us haven't had enough experience doing that throughout our careers," he said grimly.

"How long will you be gone?"

"Ten days. I told Roger to have Gloria get word to you. We'll probably have a three-day weekend when we get back. Can we go out when I get back?" he asked.

"I don't know what I'll be doing when you get back, Jake. I don't want to make promises I may not be able to keep," she cautiously answered, remembering her thought that she needed to quit seeing him.

"Well, *if* I call you when I get back and *if* you're not busy, will you go out with me?"

"Probably," she answered.

He laughed. "You feel some special need to keep me guessing?"

"No! I'm just trying to be honest."

"Okay, okay. Don't get defensive. I don't want to end our conversation on a sour note. But I really need to get back to sleep. Hope your trial goes well, and I'll call as soon as I get back to town. Good night, Claire."

"Good night, Jake," she replied and hung up the phone while inwardly chastising herself for calling.

I know I'm attracted to him, and I need to stop this relationship before it goes any further, she thought. *So why can't I keep myself from calling him,* she pondered as she walked to her bedroom.

ᨠ

The following day, the lawsuit almost ground to a stop as the defense attorney objected to almost every question Lyle posed to his first witness. It was an old tactic. Although the attorney knew his objections would be overruled, the interruptions caused a lack of continuity in the pattern of questioning. Claire observed the majority of the jurors begin to fidget and lose their focus early in the afternoon, which was disturbing to watch. Lyle's ability to question witnesses far excelled that of the opposing counsel, but his expertise was diminished by the constant delays.

Driving back from the courthouse after court had been adjourned for the day, Lyle settled into the driver's seat of the battered yellow Volkswagen.

"Tell me something, Claire. Is it me or is this trial going down the tubes before we even get a good start?" he asked as they head toward the office.

"Don't overreact," Claire answered, not wanting to further upset him.

He laughed—not just a little chuckle, but a deep, belly laugh.

"What is wrong with you?" Claire asked as he turned and headed away from the office.

"Nothing. Let's go get something to eat," he suggested, catching her by surprise.

"I probably should go home if we don't have to work late," Claire told him.

"There's certainly no need to work late tonight. I'm still questioning the same witness I started with this morning. If the rest of the trial moves at this pace, we won't be through for six months. Why do you need to go home? You'll just have to fix dinner when you get there. This way, you'll have it out of the way and won't have to do the dishes," he said, pulling the car to a stop in front of The Circle restaurant.

She immediately thought of Jake. *Stop it*, she told herself. *You've got to quit thinking about him.*

"Claire!" Lyle called, attempting to gain her attention. "You're acting like you're a million miles away. You going to get out?" he said, holding the car door open.

"Oh, yes, sorry," she said, trying to hide her embarrassment.

Immediately Lyle began discussing the day's events. "Tell me what you think is going on in that courtroom," he requested as he leaned across the table toward her.

"I'm just guessing, but it may be that Judge Hackley is paying you back for your earlier remarks at the sidebar—about wanting a change of venue. It's the only reason I can think of that he's allowing Bill to continue the interruptions. You know Hackley's reputation as well as I do, Lyle. Everyone says you'd better not cross him."

"I know what you're saying is true. I just don't like to think a member of the judiciary would impede justice," he said.

"Come on, Lyle. You know and I know that this kind of thing happens all the time. It's not pleasant to think about, but there are bad judges, and unfortunately you've drawn one of them for this trial."

"I've made objections to his ruling for the record. At least I'll have grounds for appeal, but I'm thinking about asking for a meeting in chambers before the trial begins tomorrow. If I don't have any success getting him to stop Bill's continual objections, I'm considering asking him to recuse himself."

"Lyle—that's a dangerous step. Are you sure you want to go that far? It could really backfire if he won't step down. And with that man's ego, I'd be shocked if he'd give it a minute's consideration," Claire responded, surprised at Lyle's suggested tactics.

"I know it's unusual. Of course, any time you ask a judge to recuse himself, there's the possibility of backlash. No one ever wants to admit he has any prejudices, least of all a judge. Personally, I admire any judge who can objectively look at a case and honestly say there are reasons why he or she shouldn't be the judge and then step down. Whether it's by their own initiative or when an attorney files a motion for recusal, I have to admire that kind of integrity."

"Why don't you talk to Dave about this? I think he could give you a much more discerning perspective," she suggested, not wanting to take part in a decision of this magnitude.

"How is the guardianship coming along for Mrs. Roseman?" he asked, changing the subject.

"There's going to be a hearing tomorrow."

"Don't tell me she's going to be in the courthouse!" Lyle stated, a note of panic in his voice.

"No, the hearing will be held at the annex building. Dave specifically requested it over there and Dr. Bogan is going to testify. John Ingmire said he would bring her to the hearing. Dave thought it would be best if the judge could visit with Mrs. Roseman personally."

Lyle nodded his head. "So has she questioned anyone about why she has to go to this hearing or what it's about?"

"Dave went out to her house and served the papers personally. He attempted to explain, but he doesn't think she ever understood. She thought the papers he was serving were to take her house. She kept telling him she wouldn't move, that they'd have to drown her first."

Lyle just shook his head. "Poor woman. It's too bad she doesn't have some family to help. You sure she doesn't have anybody?"

"Not from what I could find out. She told me she couldn't have kids, and Dr. Bogan confirmed that they'd never had any children. He's known her for years."

"Kind of sad when you think about it—being alone," Lyle remarked. "You have any family besides Michelle?" he asked, turning the conversation to a personal level.

"My mom is still alive, and I have a brother and sister," she answered.

"Where do they live?"

"My mom lives in Pittsburgh, my sister is in West Virginia, and my brother's up in Michigan. We're kind of scattered around. How about you?" she inquired, suddenly realizing how little she knew about Lyle.

"No, nobody. My parents are both deceased and I was an only child. I guess I do have one cousin in Oregon or Washington, but I've never met her—I'm not even sure of her name. I guess it would really be a half-cousin or step-cousin or is it first cousin—it's my mother's half-sister's daughter. So whatever that makes her, I've got one of those. Guess I'm kind of like Marian Roseman, huh?" he remarked, seemingly saddened by the thought.

"It's not as if you can't do something about being alone if you want to. You're still young. 'Find you a woman and settle down,' as the old saying goes," she advised him.

"In case you hadn't noticed, I'm attempting to do that," he replied.

"Excuse me?" It was all she could squeak out, desperately hoping she had misunderstood his comment.

"I am attempting to do something about it. I know I'm not very astute when it comes to dating or relationships, but I was hoping that you and I could explore that possibility."

"What possibility?" she asked, feeling somewhat dizzy.

"The possibility of you and I seeing each other, perhaps becoming involved—I mean getting to know each other on a personal level. We have so much in common, and I've always admired you," he said.

"You've always admired me? Lyle, you hardly notice me except when you're preparing for trial," she replied, astounded by his comments.

"That's not true. I don't mean to appear undiplomatic, Claire, but you have absolutely no idea what I notice or think about you. After this trial is over, I'd like for us to spend time together away from the office. I hope you'll at least give that prospect some thought."

When she began to speak, he held out his hand as if he were a policeman directing traffic to a stop. "Please don't answer now. I'd really like for you to think about it first."

She nodded her head in agreement. "Could I just say one thing?" she tentatively requested.

He smiled. "Sure, go ahead."

"When I first came to work for you and Dave, one of the speeches I received, even though I was a married woman, was that both of you frowned upon any type of intraoffice relationships. Do you recall anything along that line?"

"Of course I do. That speech was made for my benefit. Dave and Peggy are a solid couple. Besides, his Christian beliefs keep him on the straight and narrow; he doesn't believe in divorce. That's one of the reasons we don't handle them in our office," he explained.

"What do you mean, that speech was made for your benefit?"

"I told Dave I didn't want anyone coming to work for us with the idea she could snag a husband. That may sound pretentious, but I think there are *some* women who think the workplace is a hunting ground to find a husband. That may not be true, but it's what *I* think. You've probably heard some rumors about my past. Suffice it to say, I wasn't ready to enter the dating scene at the times we've been hiring. Consequently, that statement has been made to every applicant who has ever been hired in our office. Of course, with the exception of Josie, we haven't had to hire anyone for quite a while."

"You guys made that statement about intraoffice dating to eighteen-year-old Josie? I can only imagine what she was thinking!" Claire retorted, giving him a hearty chuckle.

"Now what's that supposed to mean?" he asked, pretending to be insulted.

"Exactly what you're thinking. You guys are old enough to be her father!"

"Only if we'd had children at a *very* early age," he countered.

"Not all *that* early," Claire said, laughing.

"It's nice to hear you laugh," he said, his voice once again becoming serious.

Claire could feel herself becoming uncomfortable. "You know, Lyle, I think there's a lot to be said about the difficulties that can arise out of intraoffice relationships. As an example, let's say that you and Gloria began to date and. . ."

"Let's just say that you and I began to date. We both know there's no possibility that Gloria and I would ever have a relationship outside the office," he interrupted.

"Well, I didn't think there was any possibility you and I would have a relationship outside the office either. But, for the sake of this conversation, we'll say that you and I begin dating. Don't you see the ramifications that could arise? If you gave me a raise that was larger than what the other staff members received, or gave me extra time off because I had been working long hours on a trial—the others might construe that to be favoritism. Even—"

"We already do those things, Claire," he said, once again interrupting her. "Raises are based upon performance, education, workload, dedication—we've never given equal raises to the staff. The concept of equality raises makes no sense to me—never has and never will. I'm a believer in performance-based raises and bonuses. As to hours off—we've always worked that the same way. If Gloria has to work overtime getting paperwork done, we reward that with time off. If you work overtime during trial—you get time off. How could it be construed as favoritism?" he argued, using his best courtroom tactics.

"Well, I truly believe that if we were dating, Josie and Gloria would be looking more closely at those perks and begin to wonder if they were being fairly distributed. Right now, there's no reason for anyone to think there's any form of favoritism," Claire replied.

"Does that mean you won't consider going out with me?" he asked.

"Maybe this is something else you should discuss with Dave," she suggested.

"You think that I should ask Dave if I can go out on a date?"

"Come on, Lyle. You know what I'm saying. Dating someone who works in the office can affect the whole business. I think he has a right to know you're giving thought to the idea. It's better to know up front if he's going to be against it," she responded. "Wouldn't you want him to show you the same consideration if the tables were turned?"

"You're right. I guess I would. But that doesn't mean I'm going to allow Dave's attitude to be the deciding factor," he quickly added.

ten

The next morning Claire was surprised when both Lyle and Dave were already at the office when she arrived. Dave gave her what she perceived as a look of foreboding as he bid her "good morning" without stopping to chat.

I'm letting my imagination get away from me again, she thought. *They've been discussing the trial and Lyle's suggestion to recuse Judge Hackley—it's got nothing to do with dating Lyle.*

As soon as she'd gotten settled at her desk, Lyle came bounding into the room, a yellow legal pad in one hand and a red expandable folder in the other.

"These are some of Dave's materials for the guardianship hearing this morning. Do you have time to go through and get things organized for him?"

"Sure, I'd be glad to. Did you talk about the recusal motion?" she asked, hoping that was *all* they'd talked about.

"Yeah. Dave said to go for it. He thinks somebody needs to confront Hackley. Otherwise, he'll continue with his Gestapo methods. We agree that if Hackley doesn't recuse himself, it will make the appeal a shoe-in. Last night after I got home, I called Dave. After talking to him, I got word to Hackley's clerk that I had some matters that needed to be taken up in chambers this morning. I'm hoping I gave them enough time to contact the jurors," he explained.

"I'm sure the jurors wouldn't mind staying home this morning. It's a gorgeous day to be outdoors working in the garden," she said while thinking of the lack of care she'd given the flowers and tomatoes that she and Jake had planted.

"Since I won't need you in trial this morning, would you

mind going along with Dave to the guardianship hearing? Mrs. Roseman knows you, and it might make her feel more comfortable. Besides, Dave thought there might be a possibility the judge would want to visit with you."

"About what? Mrs. Roseman probably won't even remember me," she stated, uncomfortable with the idea.

"Her disorientation when she was here at the office. The fact that she couldn't understand the information you presented," he said. "Nothing to worry about," he quickly added.

"Did you see my note?" Gloria asked as she walked in the front door. "I thought I was never going to see you again. I tried to call last evening about seven-thirty, but you still weren't home. Must be some trial!"

"What note?" Claire asked, disregarding the rest of Gloria's commentary.

"In the top drawer of your desk. Jake and Roger had to go to the field, and Jake couldn't get ahold of you. Roger told him I'd explain everything to you. I left a note for you to call me."

"I didn't see the note," Claire said. "But I did talk to Jake before he left for the field," she continued as she pulled open her desk drawer and saw Gloria's familiar scrawl on a piece of paper.

"Oh," Gloria stated and hesitated a moment. "When did you talk to him? He called Roger right before going to bed and said he couldn't reach you. That was the night before they were leaving for the field."

"I called him after I got home from work that night," Claire somewhat sheepishly admitted.

"So you like him, don't you?" Gloria goaded. "Come on, I know it's true—you like him—you can admit it to me."

"I like him, but I'm not sure I'll continue seeing him," Claire replied.

"Whhhhy?" Gloria whined.

"Good grief. That 'why' sounded like a horse whinnying,"

Claire replied, laughing at her friend's theatrics while she continued to organize the guardianship paperwork.

"Well, just tell me why you wouldn't continue to see him if you like him. You make absolutely no sense!"

"Because I don't want to get entrenched in a relationship. My first priorities are to my daughter and my job. My time with Michelle is so limited, especially when we get into trials. If I try to add anything else into my life, it gets too complicated."

"That's hogwash and you know it, Claire. Jake's willing to spend time with Michelle. He's proven that."

"Sure, for now, while we're in a 'getting to know you' type of relationship. But I'm certain the novelty will wear off," Claire explained. "Believe me, I'm not being judgmental. I do understand. However, being with her gives me immense pleasure; after all, she's my daughter. I don't quite know how to explain it, but when I'm with her it's like entering a peaceful oasis, a respite from the world. I realize it isn't the same for others who are around her. Even Glenn didn't understand or experience that pleasure—and he was her father. Now that God has blessed me with the ability to find joy and delight in Michelle's life, I'm not willing to compromise her future," Claire stated.

"I'm not going to argue about Michelle, but I think Jake genuinely enjoys the visits. Either that or he's giving Roger quite a line."

"How much does Roger know about Jake?" Claire asked.

"I don't know. He thinks he's a really great guy. Says he's an excellent noncommissioned officer and that good NCOs are hard to come by nowadays. Those are Roger's words, not mine," she clarified.

"Do you know how long Roger and Jake have known each other?"

"No. Why, all of a sudden, are you asking these questions?"

"I don't know. It's just that sometimes I think there's more to Jake than he tells me. I mean, I've asked about his past and he's given me the basic information, but I just have this nagging feeling there's something missing," Claire replied.

"You sure do enjoy super-analyzing people, don't you?"

"I guess. Besides, working in a law office begins to make you question everything. I think I've become pretty suspicious since I started working here."

"Obviously!" Gloria retorted.

"You finished with that file, Claire?" Dave asked as he walked into the room carrying his brief case.

"Sure am," she said as she extended the file toward him.

"Ready to go?"

"Yes," she answered, pulling her purse from the desk and grabbing a legal pad.

"What's going on? How come you're going to court with Dave instead of Lyle?" Gloria inquired, obviously confused by the change.

"I'll explain it to you later. I've got to go," Claire said, rushing to catch up with Dave, who was already waiting at the front door.

The two of them walked silently to Dave's car, and Claire found herself smiling as she slid onto the soft leather seat of the Mercedes. The comparison between Dave's plush Mercedes and Lyle's old Volkswagen was mind-boggling.

"What's the joke?" Dave asked, apparently noting her smile.

"No joke. The differences between you and Lyle just make me smile, that's all," she told him.

"Yeah, we aren't too much alike, but I love Lyle like the brother I never had. He's a good guy. I guess we need to talk about that," he said, leaving the statement hanging.

"There's nothing to talk about, Dave. I think Lyle's a good guy too. Sometimes his obsession for perfection in preparing his cases drives me a little nutty, but, other than that, I like working for both of you," she replied.

"I'm not talking about working for us. Lyle talked to me last night—about the two of you."

"There is no 'two of us,' Dave. Lyle indicated that he might be interested in seeing me socially. I told him I thought intraoffice dating could lead to difficulty, and I also suggested he talk to you. Honestly, I've never even thought about either of you guys in any other way than as my bosses," she told him.

"Peg will be relieved," he said giving her a laugh. "I hope you at least count us as friends as well as your employers."

"Well, of course, that too," she responded. "Do you think the hearing will take very long?" she asked, wanting to change the subject.

"It's hard to tell. A lot will depend upon Mrs. Roseman and how much testimony the judge will require. Judge Long is hearing the case, and he's pretty thorough."

Claire nodded and was relieved they had reached the courthouse parking lot. She didn't want to discuss Lyle, and she wished the whole situation would just go away. All of a sudden, it seemed her personal life was becoming extremely complicated—especially for someone who had no interest in a serious relationship.

Mrs. Roseman placed her hand on the Bible and took her oath. As soon as she'd been sworn in, she gave Judge Long a sweet smile and turned toward him. "I *always* tell the truth, but I did that little 'swearing-in' thing to make all of you happy," she said.

"Thank you Mrs. Roseman," he said, returning her smile and watching as she gave a childish wave toward Claire.

Claire smiled in response.

"That's the lady that's coming to live with me," Mrs. Roseman explained.

"Oh, really? Tell me about it," the judge encouraged.

"Well, she doesn't like the fact that the government is trying to take my land, so she's going to come and live with me. The two of us are going to buy shotguns, and when they come with those bulldozers, we're going to shoot 'em dead," she told him, nodding her head up and down emphatically.

Judge Long looked toward Claire and then back at Mrs. Roseman.

"When did you and—by the way, what is that lady's name?" he asked, pointing toward Claire.

"That's Mabel," she resolutely replied. "Mabel Marsden— we've known each other for years. Went to school together back in the one-room schoolhouse that used to be over by Lyndon. They tore it down a few years ago. We had a good time in school, didn't we, Mabel?"

"You know, Mrs. Roseman, I think it would be all right for you to go home now. I believe we can finish this matter without you. Would you like to go home?" he asked in a kindly voice.

"Of course I want to go home. I never wanted to leave in the first place, but John said I had to come here. I'm afraid to leave, but John promised they wouldn't bring the bulldozers while I was gone, didn't you, John?" she asked her neighbor, who was sitting on a folding chair in the small courtroom.

He shook his head up and down in agreement. Standing up, he motioned toward the woman to exit the witness box.

"I'll be seeing you later, Mabel," Mrs. Roseman said to Claire as she walked by her on the way out of the courtroom.

Dave rose from his chair.

"You may as well sit down, Mr. Wilmott," the judge said to Dave. "It's obvious this woman has some problems, but I want the doctor's testimony before I make any decision."

Dave sat down. "Told you he's thorough. No other judge would have even bothered to go any further with this," he whispered to Claire.

Judge Long instructed Dave to proceed with questioning Dr. Bogan, and by the time he had finished, there was no doubt that Mrs. Roseman's condition was worsening and there was no medication that would help. In fact, Dr. Bogan had previously made attempts to convince his patient to enter an assisted care facility for the elderly, but she always refused. It was still his recommendation that she reside in a facility where there were professional staff members who could assist her as needed.

When Dr. Bogan's testimony was completed, the judge signed the guardianship papers. He would have preferred to appoint a relative, but when Dave advised him that none could be located, he appointed a local attorney as Mrs. Roseman's guardian and conservator.

"That went easier than I expected," Dave commented as he tucked the file into his briefcase and escorted Claire back toward his car.

"I guess so. It sure is sad to see someone who's been an upstanding, contributing member of society end up like Mrs. Roseman, isn't it?"

"Yes, it is. It's even sadder that she doesn't seem to have any relatives to help out. Lyle tells me this subject came up last night when you two were talking," Dave said.

Oh, no, Claire thought. *I walked right into that one.*

"We talked about it briefly. How are Peg and the kids doing?" Claire asked, hoping to change the subject.

"Fine, fine. What else did you and Lyle discuss?" he asked, obviously unwilling to be deterred.

"I'll tell you what I told Lyle. I think it's a mistake for an employer and employee to see each other socially. It can cause friction and hard feelings among coworkers. I also pointed out to him that I had received a speech during my interview. As I recall, that speech spelled out the fact that you and Lyle were opposed to that type of socializing also. When he told me last night that he was interested in dating me, I was stunned. And just in case the thought has crossed your mind, I've never done anything to encourage him," Claire told him.

"That thought *never* crossed my mind. I know you're a fine Christian woman, Claire, and basically I agree with everything you've said. However, it has been a very long time since Lyle has shown any interest in dating. Personally, I think part of it is because of a bad experience long ago, but I think the other part is that he's been very devoted to making the business a success. I'm sure he's fearful of being hurt again, and I would hate to see that happen. However, the only way he's ever going to find the right person is to get out there and take a chance. He already knows your qualities, and there's a measure of safety with you," Dave stated.

"But I'm not interested in a committed relationship, Dave. Quite honestly, I don't know that I'd ever consider marrying again. My first priority is my daughter."

"Why does being Michelle's parent preclude remarriage? Lyle's a good man. I'm sure he could accept her," Dave said in his friend's defense.

"It's pretty involved, and I'm not sure I want to discuss it right now. So you're telling me you have no problem with Lyle dating me. You don't think it would cause problems within the office?" she asked, hoping she had somehow misunderstood his comments.

"I think it's a great idea. I hope you two hit it off and that someday I'll be best man at your wedding!" he said.

"You feeling all right?" Gloria asked as Claire walked into the office.

"Not really," she replied. "Where did those come from?" she asked, stopping in front of a glass vase containing a large arrangement of tinted daisies and baby's breath, sitting in the middle of her desk.

"Don't know. Guess you'll need to open the card," Gloria suggested, obviously enjoying the moment.

Please don't let them be from Lyle, she thought as she hesitated and then ripped open the envelope.

"They're from *Jake*," she said aloud.

"Who *else* would they be from?" Gloria asked, watching Claire tuck the card back into the envelope.

"What? Oh, I don't know. I just never thought about Jake

sending flowers," she replied.

"Well, why not?" Gloria asked, obviously confused.

"I guess because he's out in the field," she honestly replied.

"They *do* have contact with the outside world," Gloria replied, just as Lyle walked in the door.

"Is the hearing over?" Claire asked as soon as she saw him.

Looking at the bouquet of flowers on the desk, he stopped in front of her. "Do I have competition, or is it your birthday?" he asked.

Claire could feel Gloria's eyes riveted into the back of her head. "Is the hearing over? How did it go?" Claire once again inquired.

"Come on in my office; I'll give you the details," he said. "Hey, Dave, come here and listen to this," he called toward his partner's office.

"Believe it or not, Hackley recused himself," Lyle said to Dave and Claire as he closed his office door.

❧

"What's going on?" Gloria hissed at Claire as she walked back to her desk while Dave and Lyle stood in the doorway to Lyle's office.

"I'll talk to you later," Claire whispered, nodding toward Dave and Lyle.

"I'll be over to your place at seven," Gloria replied and went back to her typing.

eleven

"All right, just what is going on?" Gloria asked as she entered the back door of Claire's house at exactly seven o'clock.

"Judge Hackley agreed to recuse himself. The trial will have to start all over; the jury has been dismissed; the case will go to the bottom of this term's docket; *and* we get a much-needed breather," Claire replied as the pair seated themselves at the kitchen table. "Want some coffee or iced tea?"

"I'm not talking about the trial, and you know it, Claire! What's going on between you and Lyle? I heard that remark he made this morning about 'having competition.' Are you two seeing each other?" Gloria aggressively questioned her friend, totally ignoring the offer of liquid refreshment.

"Nothing is going on between Lyle and me," she answered while moving toward the refrigerator. "I think I'll have tea. Do you want some or not?"

"No, I don't want any tea or coffee or anything else to drink. I want some straight answers. Am I going to get them or not?" she demanded.

"Not if you talk to me in that tone of voice," Claire answered, sounding as though she were instructing a toddler.

"Okay, my apologies. *Please* tell me what is going on."

"First, let me say that I wouldn't divulge any of this to you if Lyle hadn't made that off-handed remark within your hearing," Claire began.

Gloria gave her an offended look. "Just why wouldn't you tell *me*?"

"Because until there's actually something to discuss, there's no reason to spend a lot of time on any particular subject. Besides, you know that I like my personal life to remain personal. Anyway, after we were through in court yesterday, Lyle asked me to go to dinner. Actually, he didn't wait for my agreement. We ended up at The Circle, and during the course of our conversation he asked me if I would consider seeing him on a social basis."

"You're kidding," Gloria remarked before she could go any further. "What did you tell him?"

"I explained that I thought it could cause problems for employees and employers to date. Then I reminded him of the speech he and Dave gave during my interview about being opposed to intraoffice dating, and I suggested that he probably should discuss the matter with Dave."

"What? Why should he discuss whom he dates with his law partner?" Gloria asked, giving Claire an amazed look.

"He shouldn't discuss *whom he dates*. But I think if he's going to date someone that works in the office, he should see if Dave has any objections. If it creates friction within the office, it affects both of them," Claire explained.

"You aren't seriously thinking about dating Lyle, are you?" Gloria asked.

"What's wrong with Lyle?"

"Well, nothing, I guess. I just never thought about him dating anyone. Besides, you're dating Jake," she reminded Claire.

"What has Jake got to do with any of this? I keep telling everyone that I'm not interested in a serious relationship with anyone. Occasional dating is fine, but I'm not interested in anything more than that. Unfortunately, nobody seems to hear me," she said.

"I think Jake's more your type. Besides, he likes Michelle," Gloria stated, ignoring Claire's remarks.

"For goodness sake, Gloria. Lyle doesn't even *know* Michelle. Don't you think it would cause problems if one of the guys were dating an employee?" Claire asked.

"Yeah—Dave's married, remember?"

"Cute! You know what I'm asking! Think about it—what

if I were dating Lyle and the guys decided to give bonuses. What if my bonus check were larger than yours? Wouldn't you think it was because I was dating Lyle?"

"Your bonus check is always bigger than mine, and you're *not* dating Lyle," Gloria answered.

"Are you jealous about that?" Claire inquired.

"No. You work lots more hours than I'd ever even consider working. Besides, we do different jobs. I don't make the same salary as you either, but that's because we perform different work. If you were dating Lyle, I don't think they'd give you preferential treatment. Besides, Dave wouldn't stand for it—even if Lyle were swayed by his emotions."

"You're a big help. One minute you're telling me I shouldn't even consider dating Lyle; the next minute you're telling me it wouldn't create problems within the office."

"They're two entirely separate issues. I don't think you should date Lyle, just because I don't think Lyle is the right guy for you, not because he's our boss. I think Jake is a better match," Gloria explained. "Speaking of which—Roger called me this evening, and they're going to get back from the field early. Jake wanted me to relay a message to hold the weekend open for him. Maybe the four of us can go somewhere together," Gloria suggested, her voice full of enthusiasm.

"Maybe," Claire answered, glancing at the vase of daisies she'd brought home from the office. "We'll see."

❧

Lyle had been unexpectedly called out of the office to attend top-level corporate planning sessions being conducted by Platino Corporation, one of their largest clients. Dave would have attended in Lyle's place had the land condemnation trial continued. But, clearly, Lyle was Platino's first choice, their "fair-haired boy" as Dave lightheartedly referred to him.

Upon hearing the news that Lyle would be in Kansas City the remainder of the week, Claire experienced a sense of relief. She wanted some time to evaluate her thoughts and consider the pros and cons of the dating concept. To date, the idea invoked nothing but thoughts of disaster.

Lyle had given her Friday and Monday off to compensate for the overtime she had worked while preparing for the trial. It was a beautiful day, and she was finally getting to spend some much-needed time pulling weeds out of the flower beds.

"Need some help?"

Claire jumped. She had been totally engrossed in the work and hadn't heard anyone come up behind her.

"I'm sorry. I didn't mean to startle you," Jake said, stooping down beside her and pulling at a weed.

"Guess I must have been deep in thought," she said, turning to look toward the street. "I didn't even hear you drive up."

"Hope some of those thoughts were about me," he ventured, throwing some weeds into the growing pile beside her right hand.

"Gloria said you were supposed to be back early." she said, deliberately not giving an answer to his comment.

"We were told they cut it short because performance levels were so high. I don't know if that's the real reason or not, but I'm always glad to get out of the field. Did Gloria also mention that I'd like to spend some time with you this weekend?" he asked.

"Yes, she mentioned that."

"And?"

"Well, it depends on what you have in mind, I guess. Gloria said something about all four of us getting together. You know anything about that idea?"

"Roger and I were thinking you two might like to go to Worlds of Fun. That is, if you like amusement parks. Do you?"

"Sure, I like amusement parks, but I don't ride anything that goes around in circles. Makes me sick to my stomach.

Besides, they usually have some good entertainment at Worlds of Fun, at least on the weekends," she responded.

"We were thinking about going early tomorrow morning. Gloria thought maybe we could take a picnic instead of eating in the park. Either way is fine with me," he quickly added.

"When did Gloria make all these plans?" Claire suspiciously inquired.

"Roger got back before me; sometime early this morning. He met Gloria and took her out for coffee this morning, and they discussed it. Roger gave me a call just before I left to come over here. So what sounds best to you? A picnic or eating at the park?"

"Tell you what. I'll talk to Gloria, and we'll get that part arranged. Exactly what time did you have in mind to leave?"

"We thought about eight-thirty. The park opens at ten, and it'll take us a couple hours to get there. Sound okay?"

"Sounds fine," she replied.

"Tomatoes need water?" he asked as she continued weeding.

"As a matter of fact, they do."

She didn't look up as he rose and moved away. "Your hose is missing," he called from inside the garage.

"Sorry—it's hooked up out back. I didn't put it away last time I watered," she exclaimed as he walked toward her.

"I won't give you the speech that it's really better to put things away," he joked as he walked toward the backyard. Shortly, she heard a banging noise followed by a crash.

"What's wrong?" Claire yelled, running toward the backyard. Jake was sprawled amidst the tomato plants; a metal rack and small clay pots that were used for an herb garden were scattered around him.

"Hope those didn't have anything in them," Jake remarked as he pointed toward the pots that had fallen to the ground.

"Not yet," she answered. "What happened?"

"I tripped on the hose," he replied. "*Now* you get the speech about putting things away!"

Claire couldn't help herself. She laughed until tears streamed down her face. It was just such a sight to see him lying there surrounded by all that mess. Slowly he lifted himself up, using the water spigot to lean on. She didn't notice his hand turning the handle until the hose was aimed at her, a stream of cold water causing her to let out a shriek.

"*Jake*! That's cold! Turn it off!" she screamed, running to the side of the house and finally out of the water's reach. "Look at my clothes. I'm soaking wet," she chastised him, standing just beyond the spray of water.

"You're only damp. I hardly got you at all," he said. "Come on back here," he urged.

"Oh, sure. Why would I want to come back there? So you can douse me again?"

"Okay, I quit. I'll go turn it off," he said, "but we better get this mess cleaned up."

Hesitantly, she followed and then peeked around the corner of the house until she was sure he had put down the hose. Once assured, she gingerly walked toward him while leaning down and picking up several of the small planters. As soon as she turned away, he picked up the hose, once again squirted her, and just as quickly dropped the water hose. By the time she turned around to scold him, he was directly behind her.

Just as she opened her mouth to reprimand him, he gathered her into his arms, his lips covering hers. She could feel the warmth spreading throughout her body as he held her.

"Jake, I think we should talk," Claire said, her voice serious. "Why don't you come inside?"

Grabbing a towel from the laundry room as they walked in the back door, Claire dried herself off as best she could.

"I'm sorry. I didn't realize you'd be so upset," he began.

"I'm not upset about the surprise shower," she said. "Sit down," she offered, motioning toward one of the kitchen chairs.

"I don't know how else to address this subject, except

straightforwardly. And I'm ashamed of myself for not doing it sooner. Jake, I need to know if you're a Christian."

"Well, my folks sent me to church on Sundays when I was little. Does that count?" he asked, obviously trying to make light of the subject.

"No, Jake, that doesn't count," she said.

"I'm sorry. I tend to joke around when a question makes me uncomfortable," he replied.

"So I've noticed," she responded.

He hesitated for a moment and then met her gaze. "I believe there's a God, but I realize I don't have whatever it is you've got. Believe me, Claire, I know there's something different about you. The way you've been able to accept the things that have happened in your life, the fact that you haven't turned bitter or cynical in spite of it all. You seem to have an inner peace, a kind of joy. It's what first attracted me to you and, to a certain extent, why I can't stay away from you."

"Those are very flattering statements. I'm not sure they're entirely true, but you need to know that I would never consider becoming involved with a non-Christian. When we first met, I told you I wasn't interested in a serious relationship and you told me that you weren't either. We agreed to a friendship. I'm afraid that's all I can offer," she told him.

"I see. Well, how about if I go to church with you on Sunday?"

"Going to church on Sunday is fine. You're more than welcome, but understand that going to church doesn't change anything. Walking in the door of a school doesn't create a scholar, and entering the doors of a church doesn't create a Christian. Both take desire and a willingness to have your life molded and reshaped," she told him.

"I'm willing to give it a try," he said.

"May I ask you another serious question?"

"Sure," he replied, running his fingers through his disheveled hair.

"One night when I was working late, I drove past the Odyssey Club. While I was waiting for the light to change, someone who looked like you went inside the club. Was it you, Jake? I need to know if drinking and nightclubs are a part of your life."

He stared directly into her eyes for a moment and then looked down at the floor. Slowly he raised his eyes back to meet hers. "The truth is that I do enjoy going to nightclubs occasionally and yes, I do drink—sometimes at clubs, sometimes at home. Not on a daily basis, mind you. Usually, just on weekends or nights when I don't have to get up for work the next day. And I do drink to excess."

"Frequently?" she asked.

"When I drink, it's usually to excess. I'd rather lie to you, but I know if you did a little checking, it wouldn't be difficult to find out anything I'm telling you. And I know you'd think less of me if I lied about it," he honestly answered.

"Can you stop?" she asked.

"You mean quit drinking completely? I doubt it. I've never tried—never had any desire or any reason to ever try and quit."

"I see," she quietly replied as a sick feeling began to develop in the pit of her stomach.

"Does this conversation mean that our trip is off for tomorrow?" he asked.

"I'm afraid so," she replied, wanting with all her heart to say she would still go with him, that one more date couldn't matter. But she knew it would. She knew she was falling in love with him, but she couldn't allow that to happen.

"Claire, I care about you, more than you probably realize. And you have no idea what a positive influence you've been in my life. Please don't do this," he pleaded.

"I'm sorry, Jake. Unfortunately, we moved a step beyond friendship before I asked you the basic questions that I should have asked when we first met. I take the blame for this, and if it gives you any comfort at all, this is painful for me, also," she told him.

"It doesn't make it any easier at all," he said rising from the chair. "I'm not going to promise that I'll be able to leave you alone, but I'll try," he said. "Good-bye, Claire," he said, walking out the door, his arm raised in the air with the familiar key ring hanging from his fingers.

"Good-bye, Jake," she whispered, feeling a sadness wash over her.

"Dear Father," she prayed, "help me be strong. Show me Your will; reveal Yourself to Jake and convince him to seek You."

It was a short petition, but one of the most heartfelt she had ever prayed.

twelve

"Jake got orders for Germany," Claire said to Gloria as she walked into the office on a Monday morning some four months later.

"How'd you find out?" Gloria asked. "You two still spending time on the telephone?"

"He called last night and told me he'd be leaving in a couple days. I guess he's known for a couple of months, but he didn't say anything," she replied.

"I don't understand you, Claire. You won't see the guy, but you keep talking to him on the phone."

"He says it helps keep him from going out and drinking if he can talk to me. I realize that he may hang up the phone and go to some bar as soon as we're through talking, but at least it gives me an opportunity to help in some small way. I really do care about him. Had things been different, I think he's the guy who could have convinced me it would be possible to remarry without jeopardizing Michelle's welfare."

"I'm really sorry. Maybe it'll be easier once he's away from here," Gloria said, giving her a hug. "You been dating Lyle?"

"You sure know how to switch gears in a hurry," Claire said, laughing at the question.

"Well, have you?"

"We've had a couple dates."

"Well, what do you think? Any possibilities there?"

"You never give up, do you?" Claire said, shaking her head. "He reminds me a lot of Glenn. He's so serious, and a lot of the qualities that make him a really good lawyer don't transfer all that well into a personal relationship."

"Such as?" Gloria persisted.

"He's a perfectionist. Everything has to run according to an exacting schedule. That's great stuff in a courtroom, but it doesn't produce a spontaneous evening of relaxation," Claire explained.

"Have you taken him along when you go to Michelle's?"

"No. In fact, I turned down several dates with him because I had already made plans to go see Michelle. He never asked to go along, and I never invited him. Somehow, I think he would have been uncomfortable."

"That's not fair, Claire. How can you make that kind of judgment?"

"I know it's not fair, but I don't have to worry about it now."

"What does *that* mean?"

"I told him I thought it would be better if we quit seeing each other socially. We really don't click. It wasn't just me; he realized it too. I didn't want to begin feeling uncomfortable coming to work, and that possibility existed if we continued to try and pursue something that just wasn't there," Claire said.

"You should have dated him at least a while longer. You need a social life of some kind," Gloria replied.

"It wouldn't have been fair to lead him on, Gloria. Besides, my life was just fine before you introduced me to Jake," Claire rebutted.

"So does that mean it isn't all right now?" Gloria asked.

"It's different. I'm not as satisfied, not as content with living out my life alone, yet I don't want to settle for something or someone who will only lead to disaster," she explained.

"Speaking of disaster, has Dave told you that Rutherford Insurance has hired him as their workers' compensation defense attorney for the entire state? I don't see how we're going to handle that without some additional help around here," Gloria declared.

"Lyle mentioned something about it, but I didn't realize it had gone through. He said they might hire another attorney or even a law clerk to help out," Claire informed her.

"I was thinking more along the line of another secretary! Not another attorney who will produce more work for us," she retorted.

"If it starts to get overwhelming, tell them you need help," Claire advised.

❧

Jake glanced around the apartment one last time. It had been practically empty for the past two weeks when the movers had appeared to pack the belongings that he could not carry with him. Those items, known as "hold baggage," were shipped separately. With any luck, that shipment would reach Germany before he did, although experience had taught him that it was usually delivered anywhere from three weeks to three months after signing in at a new duty assignment.

His schedule during the past few weeks had been regimented by an attempt to complete the list of activities necessary to clear one duty assignment and leave for another. Since receiving his movement orders to the U. S. Army Aviation Maintenance Support, located at Coleman Barracks in Mannheim, Germany, he had begun the out-processing regimen he'd been through so many times before.

Now, a day before he was to leave, he'd gone through Finance and received his records and travel pay; he'd been to the Personnel Office, where he received copies of the records relating to his military history. Next, he had been through the Troop Medical Clinic, where he had been poked, prodded, and finally approved as medically fit for overseas duty. His flight arrangements had been completed through the Transportation Unit, and two days earlier he had picked up the airline tickets that, to his relief, were on a commercial airline rather than military transport.

He locked the apartment door and walked downstairs to the first floor. After knocking on the door that boasted a sign indicating the "Manager," he patiently waited until the door swung open.

"Right on time, Sergeant Lindsey," the landlady said, checking her wristwatch. "That's what I like about renting to GIs—they know how to be on time," she said, holding out her hand.

"You check the apartment?" Jake asked as he handed her the key.

"Sure did. Got your deposit refund check right here," she said, handing him the draft. "You've been a good tenant. If you get orders to come back, just write me a letter, and I'll try and hold an apartment for you," she said.

"I'll do that," he replied.

Thoughts of leaving had plagued him all week. He had always looked forward to new assignments and moving on— shaking the dust off his feet. But this time was different. Although Claire had held true to her word and had not dated him any further, their long telephone conversations had caused him to reflect upon his future and his goals in life.

Claire was stable. She knew what she believed and held fast to it. He admired her straightforward explanations and willingness to share her beliefs, but he had not yet been able to find God. Not that he didn't occasionally search, especially when he was feeling particularly remorseful after a night of heavy drinking.

"It's a gift," Claire had told him when he asked how she was so assured of her salvation. "You're trying to make it too difficult, Jake," she had said. "All you need to do is believe that Jesus Christ is the Son of God, that He died for your sins, rose from the dead, and is coming again. Then just ask Him to be your Lord and Savior, and repent of your sins."

It sounded simple enough, but Claire didn't know what he was really like—only God did. Jake had wanted to tell her that salvation was easy for someone like her—what was there for God to forgive? A few small mistakes here and there. But, for someone with his past, God surely had something else in mind, some payment that had to be made before receiving His gift. He wasn't ready to make any payments—or give up his drinking.

Jake walked outside and unlocked the door of the light blue Plymouth sedan he'd rented as a means of transportation during his last week in the States. It was a poor substitute for the sporty Datsun, but cheaper than paying a taxi. A young lieutenant had purchased his "Z," as Jake affectionately referred to the vehicle, and had insisted upon taking possession earlier in the week.

Unable to stop himself, he turned the car and headed toward Claire's house. He was sure that she wouldn't be home, but somehow he couldn't resist the impulse to drive by just one last time. The house looked deserted, and Claire was obviously at work. Instead of heading toward post, he aimlessly drove through town and then onto the nearby interstate highway, his mind replaying the past months since he'd met Claire and Michelle.

He hadn't intended to come here, but subconsciously he must have been thinking about it. Because now here he was, sitting in front of the beige ranch-style house he had visited with Claire on several occasions—Michelle's house. He wasn't sure what time the girls came home from the day center, but he could see lights in the house. With the venetian blinds partially opened, he could even make out the figure of someone moving around.

Hesitantly he got out of the car, walked to the front door, and rang the doorbell. A few moments later, the door swung open.

"Well, it's been a while since we've seen you come calling," Sandra said in her cheerful tone of voice. "Get on in here; we're letting all the warm air out," she instructed, pulling him into the house. "Claire out there somewhere?"

"No, I'm alone," he replied. "I'm heading for Germany tomorrow and just wanted to stop and say good-bye to Michelle," he explained. "Is that okay? Since I'm alone, I mean," he asked, not sure what rules there might be about visiting any of the children.

"Why, sure it's okay. I'm sure Claire would be just thrilled to know you took the time to come over and see Shelly before you left. We're just getting ready to eat supper. You want a cup of coffee or a soda?" she offered, leading him into the dining room where the girls were seated around the table waiting to be fed.

"Coffee would be great," Jake answered, seating himself beside Michelle.

"You want to try and feed Michelle while I feed Beth?" Sandra asked, bringing along a dinner plate with his cup of coffee.

"I've never fed her. I'm not sure I'd know how," he replied, recalling the trip to the Village Inn.

"Just lift the spoon to her mouth, and she'll do the rest," Sandra nonchalantly replied, beginning to feed Beth.

Jake picked up the spoon, dipped it into the puréed food, and scooped up a spoonful. Lifting it toward Michelle, he was pleasantly surprised to find that her mouth was already open, anxiously awaiting the bite. By the time he had finished, Jake's sense of accomplishment was almost equal to what he'd felt the first time he'd scored a three-pointer during a high school basketball game. He felt like cheering! Michelle had eaten and she hadn't even thrown up.

"Looks like you did okay," Sandra said, eyeing the empty plate. "Most people aren't too good feeding and helping out with these kids. But you seem to do just fine. Claire's lucky she found you. How soon you coming back from overseas?" the woman inquired.

"It's a three-year assignment," he answered, offering nothing further before downing the cup of lukewarm coffee. "I'd probably better get going. Tomorrow's going to be a long day. Thanks for allowing me to stop in and visit," he said, rising from the chair. Reaching out, he tousled Michelle's short brown hair and impulsively leaned down and quickly kissed her cheek.

"Listen, now, you be sure and get yourself over here when you're home on leave," she said, walking Jake to the front door.

"Thanks, Sandra. I'll do that. Bye, Michelle," he called out, though he knew there would be no response.

Maybe that's what Claire meant when she said visiting Michelle was like a respite from the world, he thought, realizing that the visit had done much more for him than for Michelle. *It is like a peaceful oasis.*

❧

"Had any mail lately?" Gloria asked as Claire swiveled around from her desk and picked up an expandable file folder from the floor.

"The usual bills and advertisements," Claire replied. "How about you?"

"Oh, stop it, Claire!" Gloria said, giving her friend a chuckle. "You know what I'm asking. Have you heard from Jake?"

"I think I've had the few letters I'm going to get."

"Why don't you write again? What could it hurt? After all, he must care about you and Michelle. I still can't get over his going to see her before he left. And without you! You have to admit there's something special about a guy who would do that," Gloria persuasively argued.

"I agree that he's a nice guy and it was *extremely* kind of him to visit Michelle. I told him that when I wrote. But I also told him I wouldn't participate in a one-way correspondence. He's not written further, and I don't intend to write again until I receive another letter. Besides, we're worlds apart in our beliefs. I don't think Jake is willing to change, and I know I'm not! So I've just got to believe that God is at work in this. And at this point, I'd say God isn't leaning toward a relationship between Jake and me," Claire replied, giving her friend a consoling smile.

"Did you ever think that maybe you expect too much in a man?" Gloria inquired.

"Well, look who's talking, Miss Never-Been-Married. Aren't you the girl who's always telling me you're not tying the knot until Mr. Perfect arrives on the scene?" Claire questioned with a giggle.

"We're not talking about me, Claire. You just quit changing the subject—this is about you. I'm trying to be serious. How many guys do you think are going to be willing to take on the responsibility you've got with Michelle?"

Claire's face quickly lost all traces of humor. "I'm going to be serious too, Gloria. That child is *mine,* and I don't need or expect anybody else to *take on* that responsibility. I'm not looking for a husband, and I'm certainly not looking for a surrogate father for Michelle. We're doing just fine the way we are. Maybe this is a subject we should consider closed before it affects our friendship."

The impact of Claire's statement was obvious. Gloria's usual bronze complexion had faded several shades, and her lips were quivering while tears threatened to spill over and run down her cheeks at any moment.

"I would never intentionally do anything to jeopardize our friendship, Claire. It's because I care about you so much that I push. I'll never mention the subject again, I promise. Please accept my apology," she said, her words difficult to understand amid the sniffles and intermittent sobs.

"Of course I accept your apology," Claire said, embracing her friend. "And I'm sorry I was so harsh. I didn't intend to make you cry. Well—maybe just a little," she said, causing both of them to laugh.

thirteen

Gloria's observation that Rutherford Insurance would monopolize various resources of the small law firm proved to be true. The Rutherford account soon became a major part of the law practice, and because Dave didn't like to be away from his family, Claire was thrust into the position of traveling throughout the state to investigate claims. On most occasions, she also filled the role of office representative at the bimonthly executive meetings held at the Rutherford Insurance headquarters in Kansas City. For the first several months she had accompanied Dave, but soon it became evident that Claire was the one with the statistical information the company wanted. After that, Claire attended the meetings while Dave spent his time appearing at court hearings and depositions. She was enjoying the challenge of being involved in a new aspect of their thriving law practice, although the time away from home was also beginning to place an unwanted burden upon her.

It was a cold mid-February day, and the wind had picked up just as she was leaving the house. The clouds were an ominous gray that threatened to dump snow showers upon them at any moment. Pulling on her calf-length tan leather coat, Claire tucked a heavy scarf and her unlined leather dress gloves into her briefcase. The gloves looked good, but they didn't give her the warmth she would need today.

The short walk to the garage made her wish that she had chosen to wear the lined wool slacks that matched her suit jacket, instead of the skirt. *Oh well,* she thought, *I don't have time to change now, and Mr. Merickson would probably find slacks offensive even if they are part of an expensive suit.*

After throwing her briefcase and an overnight bag onto the

back seat of the car, she started the engine and backed out of the garage. The clouds remained gray throughout the drive, but at least there was no precipitation. Her plan was to remain in Kansas City, shop for some spring clothes for Michelle if the meeting at Rutherford Insurance didn't take too long, and then remain in the city overnight.

"Claire! It's good to see you," John Merickson, the Chief Executive Officer of the Midwest division, greeted as she walked into the main conference room of the plush offices.

Claire never ceased to be amazed at the opulent surroundings of the insurance company. The leather couches and chairs of varying shades of tan and brown seemed to beg visitors to sink into their lush comfort when entering the reception area; the solid mahogany desks of the duel receptionists were polished to a mirror-like sheen; and the fresh flowers that were replaced on a daily basis were obviously flown in from Hawaii or some exotic island in the Caribbean.

"Good morning, Mr. Merickson," Claire replied as the glass doors swung closed behind her.

"Let me take your coat," he offered, lifting it from her arm and carrying it out to one of the receptionists.

She sat in her usual place, which was the chair to Mr. Merickson's left. Sinking into the leather executive chair, one of twelve that surrounded the oak conference table, she began pulling files from her briefcase as the rest of the personnel drifted into the conference room.

Claire no longer felt intimated or uncomfortable in the Rutherford conference room. She'd attended enough meetings that it was becoming second nature. There was one female executive who was a member of the board, Janice Richmond; the remainder were men. Mr. Merickson assigned seats to each person attending the meetings, and unless he asked someone to switch, everyone was expected to be in the same chair at subsequent meetings.

Harvey Leonard had always sat across from Claire and to

Mr. Merickson's right—until today. Claire had just lifted her head to say good morning to Harvey, when the seat was filled by a man she'd never seen before. His dark hair was wavy and slightly graying at the temples, and he sported a neatly trimmed mustache, which also showed a hint of gray. He appeared to be tall, although she couldn't tell for sure since he had already seated himself before she caught a glimpse of him. He was impeccably dressed in a black pin-striped suit, a gray shirt that appeared to be the exact color of his eyes, and a black and gray striped silk tie. He wore no jewelry except silver cuff links engraved with the initials HTA in each of the French cuffs of his long-sleeved shirt.

He's quite a contrast from Harvey Leonard, Claire thought as John Merickson called the meeting to order.

"First of all, for any of those who haven't yet been told, Hugh Anderson is the new director of our workers' compensation division," he said, smiling toward the man sitting to his right.

"Claire, I know this comes as a surprise to you, but Harvey was promoted and is moving to our Connecticut offices. I hope you and Hugh will develop the same fine working relationship that existed between you and Harvey," he said.

Claire's eyes locked with the gray set of eyes across the table. He grinned. *Who, besides a movie star, has a name like Hugh?* she thought, although the name somehow seemed to fit him. She returned his look, nodding in recognition.

The meeting moved along at a snail's pace, and Claire could feel herself beginning to fidget.

"You in a hurry?" Mr. Merickson asked, observing her as she glanced at her watch.

Embarrassed, Claire gave him a half-hearted smile. "A little concerned about the weather," she lamely replied.

"No need to be. It's not going to snow. My left leg always bothers me when it snows, and it feels just fine today. Besides, I want you to join several of us for a strategy meeting this afternoon after lunch. Didn't Dave mention it?"

"No, but I'm sure it merely slipped his mind," she answered, settling back in her chair. *So much for shopping. Wait until I get my hands on Dave,* she thought while returning Mr. Merickson's warm smile.

"Why don't why go over to Houlihan's for lunch?" Mr. Merickson suggested after adjourning the meeting shortly before noon. "Their onion soup with that stringy melted cheese on top sounds wonderful on a cold day like today."

"I hope you aren't planning to walk. It's too cold for that," Hugh remarked.

"Oh, I guess we could drive if you're going to be a sissy about a little cool breeze," Mr. Merickson replied, giving Claire a wink.

"Why don't you and Claire go ahead and get a table? I can finish up a few things here, and then I'll join you. Besides, you can begin showing him the ropes if you get seated before I arrive," Mr. Merickson added, looking toward Claire. "This is a bright lady. I'd steal her away from those lawyers if I thought I could get her to come here," he continued, this time directing his remarks to Hugh.

"I'll get my coat," Claire stated, embarrassed by the statement and hoping to escape before Mr. Merickson said anything further to Hugh.

"Here, let me help you with that," Hugh said, coming up behind her just as she'd begun to shove her arm into one of the coat sleeves.

"Thanks," she murmured while leaning down to pick up her purse. Removing her gloves from the soft brown leather briefcase, she walked beside Hugh toward the elevator, pulling on first one glove and then the other and watching as both receptionists carefully monitored her escort's every step.

Hugh's car was parked in the executive section of the parking garage, his name painted in block-style print along the concrete wall in front of his vehicle.

"This is it," he said, pointing toward a sleek, black Cadillac sedan.

"Big car," Claire commented but then felt ridiculous for making such a remark.

"For a single guy? Or am I reading into your thoughts?" he asked.

"Big car for anybody," she answered. "But now that you mention it, it *is* a big car for a single guy."

"I have my children with me part of the time and I need the extra space for them. And, when the weather doesn't appear cooperative, I prefer this car to my smaller one," he told her, nonchalantly.

"So you have children?" Claire pursued.

"Three. Two boys and a girl. Tim is a sophomore in college; Mike is a senior in high school; and Melissa is in ninth grade. They live in Colorado with their mother."

"Sounds like a nice family," Claire replied.

"We're divorced," he stated. "My wife and I, that is. My job required me to be gone from home frequently. She found someone else to take my place who didn't have to travel," he continued.

Claire shifted in her seat. "The Plaza always looks a little dejected after the holidays. Don't you think?" she asked.

"Is the recitation about my personal life making you uncomfortable?" he asked as he adeptly parallel parked the lengthy vehicle a short distance from the entrance to Houlihan's.

"Nice job," Claire commented under her breath.

"Thanks," he replied, letting her know he'd heard the remark. "Looks like we got here just early enough to beat the lunch crowd," Hugh stated as they walked into the quaint Irish restaurant known for its excellent cuisine and atmosphere.

"We'll need a larger table," Hugh told the waiter as he led them toward a small alcove with a bench seat facing the crowd. "Unfortunately, we'll need something that will seat at least three people, although I'd much prefer this."

Upon hearing the remark, Claire leveled a disapproving stare in his direction, but he seemed undaunted. "I've always liked those alcove tables. Even though they face out into the crowd, somehow they seem intimate. Don't you think?" he continued unabashedly, although the waiter seemed oblivious to his statements, and Claire was attempting to ignore him.

"Did I embarrass you?" he asked as soon as the waiter had placed menus in front of them and walked away.

"Yes. Quite frankly, I don't describe seating in a restaurant as intimate—especially with someone I don't even know. And I might point out that you don't know that waiter, and you *certainly* don't know me!"

He gave her a hearty laugh that caused people at several tables to turn and stare in their direction. Claire glared across the top of her menu. "Do you enjoy being the center of attention, Mr. Anderson?"

"I don't particularly mind one way or the other," he replied. "I don't let what other people think intimidate my actions. If I want to laugh, I laugh. If I want to cry, I cry. It's that simple, Miss Winslow—or may I call you Claire? I'd prefer that you call me Hugh, by the way," he added. "Ah, there's John," he said rising from his chair and motioning to the older gentleman.

"You two ordered yet?" John asked as he seated himself between the couple and immediately began discussing his concerns regarding the recent changes in the workers' compensation statutes. "When we meet next week, I want you prepared to discuss all the ramifications of those new statutes the legislature pushed through last month. There was a roll call vote on all the enactments, and I want to see how every member of the House and Senate voted on those measures," he told Claire, obviously upset over the changes.

"Next week?" Claire asked, turning toward John Merickson.

"Didn't Dave tell you we'd need to have you here for the week? I've made reservations for you at Crown Center.

Nothing like a week in the city to get rid of those winter doldrums, right?"

"Right," Claire replied with waning enthusiasm, wondering when the plans had been made and why Dave hadn't discussed them with her.

Each time Hugh attempted to turn the conversation away from business, John would quickly return to the topic, until Hugh eventually gave up. By the time they left the restaurant, Claire had listened to enough discussion of Rutherford Insurance Company to last several weeks and longed for peace and quiet. Instead, however, the three of them returned to the corporate offices to continue their conference.

By four o'clock their afternoon session was grinding to a halt, and Claire was exhausted. Gone were her plans for an afternoon of shopping and spending the night. Now her only thoughts involved getting on the highway before the five o'clock traffic jam and making a quick return home.

"It was a pleasure meeting you, Claire, and I was pleased when John said you'd be returning next week," Hugh said, extending his hand.

"Thanks," Claire replied, already dreading the thought of being away from home for a full week. *I can't wait to get home and call Dave*, she thought while following the men out of the conference room.

Hugh was standing at the conference room door holding her coat as she left the room. "I'll walk you to your car," he offered as she buttoned her coat and picked up her briefcase.

"Don't bother yourself. I can find my way," she replied rather brusquely.

"It's no bother," he answered. "Besides, we wouldn't want John to think we're not getting along, would we?" he whispered as he took her arm and led her to the elevator. Claire felt a shiver run down her spine. Hugh Anderson, she decided, was a poor replacement for Harvey Leonard.

"What's that old saying about a Ford?" Hugh asked as

Claire unlocked the car door. "F-O-R-D, fix or repair daily. That's it, isn't it?" he asked, laughing at the old cliché.

"Perhaps to some folks. To me it means afFORDable," she rebutted and slid behind the wheel. "Good-bye, Mr. Anderson," she stated as she turned the ignition and pulled out of the parking garage.

I'll take a Jake Lindsey over a Hugh Anderson any day, she thought, carefully maneuvering the car into the oncoming traffic. *That guy gives me the creeps.*

❧

"Just wait until I get my hands on Dave," Claire spouted as she walked into the office early the next morning. "Is he in there?" she asked Gloria, nodding toward his office.

"Not yet. But guess what?"

"I'll tell you what. Dave is going to be on his own with the Rutherford account if he doesn't start clueing me in on what's going on. I don't like being told I'm committed to a whole week in Kansas City when I don't know anything about it. And this new guy that Merickson hired is really something. Talk about being full of yourself—this guy puts new meaning. . ."

"Yeah, but guess what?" Gloria interrupted.

"Oh, for goodness sake, Gloria, what?" Claire asked, exasperated that she couldn't at least vent her frustrations without being interrupted.

"Jake called."

"What?" Claire asked, suddenly sitting down at her desk.

"Jake called. Yesterday while you were gone. He wanted to talk to you and said it was serious. He wouldn't tell me what it was about, but he wanted to know when he could reach you. I told him you were going to stay over in Kansas City, and I thought you'd be back Friday. By the way, what are you doing here? Didn't you say you were going to shop and spend the night?"

"Yes, but the meeting lasted all day, so I decided to come

home instead. What else did he say?"

"Nothing, honest. I tried to get him to talk to me, but he just said to tell you he had called and that he'd call again when he got a chance."

"But he said it was serious?"

"Yeah, and he didn't joke around or anything. Didn't ask about Roger or the guys at the company. Just you and Michelle. He wanted to know if you were okay and how Michelle was doing."

"He didn't sound like he'd been drinking, did he?" Claire asked.

"No, he just sounded kind of sad. Maybe depressed or something—not like the old Jake."

"Good morning, ladies," Dave called out as he entered the reception office and began stomping snow from his shoes. "How's everyone today? How was your trip to Kansas City, Claire? I thought Gloria said you weren't coming back until Friday. Couldn't stand to be away from us, huh?" he joked, the collar of his tweed overcoat turned up around his neck.

"There were a few things that mystified me, and I thought maybe we needed to have a heart-to-heart discussion. That kind of talk is better in person, don't you think?" Claire asked, watching his face for any reaction.

He turned, hung his coat on a hanger, and then carefully placed it in the closet. Claire's eyes remained riveted on him. "You have to understand, Claire," he began as he rotated toward her. "Mr. Merickson wouldn't take 'no' for an answer. He wants you there for a week. . ."

"Why didn't you at least tell me before I left?" she asked. "Didn't you think he'd mention it? When were you going to tell me, Dave—the day before?" she asked accusingly.

"I knew you'd object to a week, but I'd already agreed to it. I thought maybe Lyle could persuade you. I didn't get to talk to him until a couple of nights ago, and he said it was my obligation to tell you since I'd struck the agreement.

Some partner," he said, giving her an unpersuasive smile. "He doesn't want to do my dirty work."

"How about *your* taking a week and going to Kansas City, Dave? How inviting does that sound to you?"

"I don't like being away from my family," Dave replied.

"Well, neither do I," Claire countered.

"I'll go," Gloria interrupted. They both turned and simultaneously glared at her. "Just a suggestion," she jokingly added and then quickly went back to work.

"Let's discuss this in my office," Dave requested, walking toward the door.

"*Where* we discuss it won't change how I feel," Claire replied as she followed him and closed the door. Settling herself into one the of chairs opposite Dave's desk, she rubbed her finger along the upholstery tacks running the length of the chair arm and then looked up to meet his eyes. "Dave, I know you love your family and want to stay home, but this is *your* business, not mine. I don't like being out of town all the time, either. I realize that Michelle isn't living at home, but what if something happens while I'm out of town? I'm frightened I won't be able to be there for her if she needs me. At least you have Peg at home with the children when you're gone. I'm supposed to be teaching a Bible study class once at week at the church, but I've had to call on a substitute for three of the last five weeks. My commitments are important to me, and I'm just not willing to be gone running the Rutherford account," she stated as boldly as possible with the looming realization that losing her job would cause her personal financial disaster.

"You know, Claire, I'd like to tell you that I really don't care what you do or don't like. That I'm the boss and if I want you to go to Kansas City, you will go to Kansas City or you will find another job. But we both know that won't happen. You're a valuable employee, and deep inside, I know I've been taking advantage of you. The only reason I didn't talk to you about the week in Kansas City was that I knew you wouldn't want to go, and I felt guilty because I'd already made the commitment to Merickson," he told her.

"I appreciate your honesty, Dave. It's hard to argue with the truth. And I know that there are lots of bosses out there that would tell me to hit the road. Subconsciously, I suppose I was counting on your Christianity to save me from the unemployment line."

"I'm afraid I haven't been exhibiting my Christianity very well where you're concerned," he said, with a hint of embarrassment in his voice. "I guess the first step in solving this problem would be for you, Lyle, and me to discuss the matter in depth. Then we can decide whether we should keep the Rutherford account and, if so, how we're going to do it. Why don't we try and get together when Lyle comes back from the courthouse, say around eleven o'clock," he requested.

Claire nodded and rose from the chair. "Thanks, Dave," she said, *and thank you, Lord,* she silently prayed as she walked out of the room.

"Get things settled?" Gloria asked as Claire walked back into the office.

"We haven't even begun to get it worked out. I'm supposed to meet with Lyle and Dave later this morning. I hope that the three of us can reach some type of resolution. If we don't get it settled, I can see myself out of town all the time. As it is, I'm gone at least two nights a week traveling all over the state and then going to the meetings in Kansas City on top of that. It's just too much," Claire explained.

"You're preaching to the choir," Gloria said, giving her friend a smile. "I said Dave wasn't playing fair a long time ago, remember?"

"Yes, I do remember. I guess I didn't realize how this thing was going to mushroom."

"If you ask me, this is just too small an office to be handling that large of an account. I never did understand why

Rutherford chose a small firm in Junction City. After all, we're almost two hundred miles away. You'd think they would want one of those big Kansas City law firms, wouldn't you?"

"I wondered the same thing, but it all boils down to money. We give them several monetary advantages that they wouldn't receive from a big Kansas City firm," Claire stated.

"Like what?" Gloria inquired, leaning forward and resting her folded arms across the top of her desk.

"Our hourly rate is lower, for one thing, especially when they use a paralegal. Even Lyle and Dave don't charge the hourly rate of a typical Kansas City firm. Also, our locale is really an asset for them. Most of the companies that Rutherford insures are outside of the metropolitan area. I don't have to travel as far to investigate claims as a Kansas City-based attorney. On most trips, an attorney who lived in Kansas City would stay out overnight. I can make it back home—even if it is close to midnight."

"So they're willing to put up with the inconvenience of having out-of-town representation," Gloria replied.

"What inconvenience? We're at their beck and call. Most of the litigation ends up in this part of the state and farther west, not Kansas City. I'm there for all of their meetings, and John Merickson knows that his calls are a priority. I don't think they'd ever begin to get the same kind of treatment from a big Kansas City firm that we're giving them," Claire explained.

"One thing about it, Claire, that account sure has stabilized the income of this office. We don't have to worry about settling big cases to pay the bills or about having enough money to front the expenses to defend someone. The financial management has run a lot more smoothly with those Rutherford checks coming in every month."

"I know," Claire replied almost apologetically. "That's one of the reasons I'm so concerned about this whole thing. I know Dave and Lyle have become dependent on that money."

"Among the three of you, someone is bound to come up with a solution," Gloria remarked encouragingly. "I'd better get these pleadings done, or I'm going to be in hot water. Lyle's expecting to go over the first drafts when he gets back."

Claire sat staring at her desk for a few moments, knowing she wouldn't regain her ability to concentrate until after the discussion with her bosses. The ringing phone on her desk startled her out of the drifting course her mind had taken. Picking up the receiver, she automatically grabbed a pencil and paper, poised to write down any necessary information.

"Hello."

"Claire? This is Sandra. Sandra over at Michelle's house," she continued when there was no response.

"Oh, yes, Sandra. Is anything wrong? Is Michelle sick?"

"Everything's just fine, and so is Michelle. We're having a little party on Saturday, kind of a belated Valentine's Day party, and wondered if you'd like to join us?"

"I would love to. I was planning on coming over on Saturday to take Michelle to see *The Muppet Movie*. How about if we take all the girls?"

"Sounds like a plan to me," Sandra said. "Shelly will be on cloud nine for a week if she gets to see a movie with those Muppet characters. If she thinks seeing their show for an hour once a week on television is good, wait until she sees that big screen full of Muppets for a full-length movie," Sandra said. "What time does the movie start?"

"Either one-thirty or four o'clock. Which works better for you?" Claire asked.

"One-thirty. Lunch will be over, and we'll still have plenty of time to get to the theater ahead of time. Why don't you meet us at the theater?" Sandra suggested.

"Sounds great. I'll stop and pick up some Dairy Queen afterwards—strawberry sundaes. They're red and white and ought to fit in with the Valentine's Day theme."

Sandra laughed. "I think the Valentine's party has turned

into a Muppet extravaganza."

"Do you mind?" Claire asked, realizing that she had pushed aside Sandra's idea in favor of her own.

"You know better than that. When there's something these girls enjoy doing, I'm all for it. Besides, we both know they're going to enjoy that movie more than any party I can dream up. We'll have a great time."

"Thanks, Sandra. I'll see you Saturday," Claire said, hanging up the phone just as Lyle walked in the door.

"Got those pleadings done, Gloria?" he asked while shedding his overcoat. "Hi, Claire. How was Kansas City?" he asked, without waiting to hear Gloria's answer.

"It was full of surprises," she said quietly.

He gave her a grim smile and walked toward Dave's office. "Anyone in there with him?"

Claire shook her head and watched as Lyle walked into his partner's office. About the time Claire decided that they were going to eliminate her from the discussion, her intercom rang.

"You want to come in here?" David asked as soon as she'd answered the call.

"If you'd have kept on dating Lyle, this wouldn't have become a problem. He would have put a stop to all your traveling a long time ago," Josie declared as she sorted through the mail.

"That's no reason to date someone. Besides, who told you I ever dated Lyle?"

"Whoops," the younger girl said, casting a glance toward Gloria.

Claire shook her head at the two of them as she walked toward Dave's office. She stood in front of the door for just a few seconds. *Lord, give me the right words to say. You know how much I need this job; You know how much I dislike the traveling; and You know what's best for me. I'm placing my trust in You, Lord, knowing that whatever happens will be for the best. Thank you for your abiding love. Amen.*

"Sit down, Claire," Lyle offered, indicating the chair she'd occupied earlier that morning.

"I was beginning to think you two had reached a solution without me," she nervously stated.

"Well, I don't think we've reached a solution, but we've hashed around some of the obvious problems with keeping the account as well as the possibility of dumping it," Lyle responded. "Quite frankly, Rutherford Insurance gives us financial security during the lean times as well as providing us with the latitude to accept cases that we might otherwise be forced to pass up. I think it would be a grievous error to dump the account."

Claire felt her stomach lurch. Lyle was taking a stand directly against her.

"I have to say that I'm not willing to give up the account either, Claire," Dave quickly asserted. "That is the one clear-cut decision we have made thus far. We are going to keep the Rutherford Insurance account."

"Have you decided *how* you're going to keep it?" Claire quietly asked, looking first at Lyle and then toward Dave.

"No. That's the hard part, and you need to be a part of that discussion," Lyle replied. "We've discussed several ideas. This is really Dave's account, and I have limited expertise in the area. . ."

"Not that you couldn't learn it in a heartbeat, if you were so inclined," Dave quickly interjected.

"That's true. I could learn it. But we both know it's not an area of the law I'm interested in practicing, Dave. That's why *I* didn't negotiate with Rutherford Insurance to become their counsel," Lyle replied tersely. "I don't believe I've ever asked you to take over any of my clients, and one of the reasons we became partners was that we enjoyed practicing in different areas of the law. Our diversity was our strength."

"It's true that you haven't asked me to take over any of

your clients, Lyle. On the other hand, you don't ever handle an account that sends us a monthly paycheck the size of the Rutherford account," Dave rebutted.

"Well, I think if you'll look at the ledgers, you'll find that my litigation over the past five years has brought in a lot more than the Rutherford account will bring in over a five-year period," Lyle defended.

"Would that be net or gross?" Dave bluntly questioned.

"We recover expenses in seventy-five percent of my cases, and you know it," Lyle angrily replied, rising from his chair.

"I don't think we're accomplishing a whole lot toward resolving this problem, gentlemen," Claire interrupted, pained by the outburst she had just witnessed.

Lyle turned to say something but instead plopped into the chair next to Claire. "She's right. I apologize, Dave. I'm just looking for an easy way out, which is for you to take over the account and let me keep doing what I love."

"Sounds great if you can get it," Dave said, giving him a laugh. "I'm sorry too, Lyle. What we need is a solution, not more problems."

"Well, Claire, you know what *we* want, and you know what *you* want. Any ideas on how to solve this one?"

"You willing to spend a little money?" she asked.

"How much is a *little?*" Dave asked.

Ignoring Lyle's initial question, she forged ahead with her proposal. "When you first took this account, there was talk that you might hire another attorney or perhaps a law clerk or another paralegal." Claire watched as they both began to squirm uncomfortably at her suggestion. "I'm not talking about hiring someone full-time," she quickly added. "But what about hiring an investigator to do the fieldwork investigating the claims? If a difficult claim arose, one of you could assist. Meanwhile I'd be willing to continue the trips to Kansas City to meet with the company, if you wanted, and to travel to inspect policyholders' facilities when the need arises—as long as it doesn't get out of hand. That part of the traveling has been minimal in the past. I don't think Mr. Merickson cares who's actually working the claims as long as the investigations are conducted well. What do you think?"

They both stared at her for several minutes and then looked at each other and nodded.

"I think this might work," Lyle said, grinning at Dave and then toward Claire.

"Where are we going to find a good investigator?" Dave asked. "We're not going to find someone we can rely on—not like Claire."

"Dave! I'd love to think I'm indispensable, but let's be realistic. If I can do this, so can someone else—probably quite a few someone else's. What we need is an individual with good investigative skills that can be adapted to this type of work. There are retired policemen, retired military police, fire investigators that work twenty-four hours and are off forty-eight hours—any of those people would probably be delighted to have part-time work."

"She's a genius," Dave said to Lyle while pointing his finger toward Claire. "I'm glad we hired this one!"

"So am I," Lyle replied. "So am I."

"Thank you for your vote of approval, gentlemen. Just remember how much you appreciate me the next time I ask for a raise," Claire said with a laugh.

"There's still one problem to resolve before you walk out of here," Dave said while motioning Claire to sit back down.

"What's that?"

"Next week. I promised Merickson you'd be there next week, remember?"

"I'd almost forgotten," Claire replied. "I'll go if I have your word you won't do this again."

"You've got it," Dave answered, his face beaming. "Why don't you write up an advertisement for the investigator position so that we can get it in the newspaper right away?"

"If you're smart, you'll let her do the hiring," Lyle said, walking toward the door and holding it open for Claire.

"It would be a pleasure!" she replied. "I'll be sure to find someone who loves to travel," she replied, noticing Dave's sheepish grin.

❧

Claire leaned down to pick up the day's mail, which lay fanned out underneath the mail slot in the front hallway of her house. Turning over the envelope, she immediately recognized Jake's half-written, half-printed scrawl. "That's strange," she reflected aloud. "I didn't think I'd get a letter so soon after his telephone call to the office. I figured he was calling to apologize for not writing," she continued to herself as she tore open the envelope and walked back into the living room.

Sitting down on the red and beige floral sofa, she unfolded the single page of lined notebook paper and read. When she had finished the letter, she realized why Jake had telephoned. It was probably better she had been gone when the call arrived. A tear slid down her cheek as she slowly went down on her knees in front of the couch and fervently prayed. *Dear Lord, he's searching for You. Hear his cry, help him through this time, and make him into the man You would have him be.* She knew prayer was the only thing that was going to help Jake, and she committed herself to fervently pray for him. And pray she did—genuine, heartfelt prayers beseeching God to lead Jake throughout the painful weeks that lay ahead.

Several days later as she sat in her hotel room in Kansas City, Claire pulled out a sheet of stationery and began a letter to Jake. She told him about the successful Valentine's Day party and trip to see *The Muppet Movie* with Michelle over the past weekend, detailing the whole event; she told him of her recent encounter with the bosses and the fact that she wouldn't be traveling as much; she told him of the latest trial that Lyle would be handling and her excitement that she would once again be able to assist him; then she told him of her sorrow that his assignment in Germany had led to an Article 15 disciplinary action for his inappropriate behavior. And then she told him of her happiness that he had finally accepted Jesus as his Lord and Savior and was facing his responsibility in admitting and resolving his problem with alcohol.

Her hand almost trembled as she wrote the words "problem with alcohol." Jake hadn't used those words. Instead, he had been brutally honest. *I'm an alcoholic,* he had written. The idea that she had even considered having a relationship with an alcoholic shook her to the core. *Why didn't I realize it? How do you know someone that well and not realize he's an alcoholic?* she thought to herself. *He was a responsible citizen, worked every day, fought for his country—how could he be an alcoholic?* The questions raced around in her mind—no answers—just questions.

Claire leaned back in the chair and shook her head. "Guess I'm not a very good judge of character, Lord," she prayed aloud, "but I never thought he'd really turn his life over to You. And to tell You the truth, I still have this nagging doubt that maybe he's not sincere. But I'll keep on praying and trusting, Father, because we both know that Jake's a good man—not the man for me—but a good man."

She signed and carefully folded the letter, and then placed it in the envelope. "I'm praying for you, Jake. I hope you're doing your part," she said to the four pale green hotel walls surrounding her.

fourteen

Jake surveyed the group of people encircling him. He'd been with this treatment group for the past six weeks. They had progressed from the perfunctory denials and misplacement of blame to accepting and addressing their problems in a straightforward, honest manner. It hadn't been an easy six weeks, and he still had two more to go before "graduation."

"Okay, Jake. Let's hear what you've got to say," Bill, the group leader, ordered.

Each week the members were asked to recount their life history. Jake had been amazed at how much the members' stories had changed since those first weeks of counseling and therapy had begun. He knew that his story, also, had been tremendously modified as he began accepting responsibility for his actions and dealing with years of unresolved anger. He had used it as justification for his drinking, and it had turned into a vicious circle that had almost ruined him.

"Today, I'd like to talk about my future," Jake said, looking at Bill. "Is that okay?"

"It's okay with me. How about the rest of you?" Bill inquired, looking around the circle.

Everyone nodded in agreement, and several gave him an encouraging smile. "When I gave you my history, I talked about a woman I'd met before coming to Germany. Her name is Claire. I've decided I'm going to ask her to marry me," Jake told the group.

One of the women in the group, a young lieutenant, sat up straighter in her chair. "Isn't this the same woman who told you to take a hike?" she asked.

"She told me that she wouldn't date me because I wasn't a

Christian and because I drank," Jake defensively replied. "I never asked her to marry me."

The group laughed.

"If she wouldn't even date you, it's a pretty good bet she wouldn't have agreed to marriage," one of the men piped up. His remark lessened Jake's tension, and he laughed along with the rest of them.

"I guess you're right," he agreed. "But I've written to her and explained my situation. She wrote back, and I know she's been faithfully praying for me and my recovery. I'm getting my life in order. I really believe she cares for me."

"Well, I think you're setting yourself up for failure," another member of the group chimed in. "Just because she's praying for you doesn't mean that she's willing to marry a drunk."

"That's right," another agreed. "If she says 'no,' you'll probably end up on a binge. I think it's a stupid idea."

"Thanks for that vote of confidence," Jake replied dejectedly.

"You need to give some thought to what they're telling you, Jake," Bill counseled. "It's hard to hear opposition when you've obviously made up your mind about this idea. But you need to listen and weigh this out. There *is* a possibility that if this woman rejects you, it could set you off on a binge. I'd like to think that's not true, but you're going to be extremely vulnerable. You won't have a support system around, and those old feelings of anger and rejection can creep back in pretty quickly. I'd like you to give this some additional deliberation. Next week we'll hash it around some more. In short, I don't want you leaving the program until we've decided upon a plan," he cautioned.

Jake nodded his agreement and attempted to focus on the remainder of the meeting although by the time they adjourned, he realized that his thoughts had been on Claire rather than the discussion.

"Jake!" Bill called as the group began to disperse. "Wait up a minute. I'll walk over to the hospital mess hall with you."

"Hope you weren't too discouraged by the group's reaction," Bill said as he caught up with Jake.

"Doesn't sound like anyone has much confidence in my ability to stay sober," he replied while they walked. "This is my first visit to Stuttgart," he told Bill, attempting to change the subject.

"Well, I can think of better ways to get here than signing in to the patient treatment facility," Bill said, giving him a pat on the back. "Jake, you're doing an excellent job in the program, and I don't think the comments that were made today were designed to discourage you. But there is always a concern when an alcoholic must deal with unexpected rejection or a devastating problem right after leaving treatment. I think the group is concerned that you may be setting yourself up for failure. And you must remember that we're supposed to speak honestly. If nothing else, the members of your group have learned that lesson well!"

"I think I'm right about this, Bill. I love Claire, and I want to marry her," he insisted.

"Tell you what—on rare occasions, I break the rules around this place. I know you're not permitted telephone calls until next week, but I'm going to consider this as a part of your treatment program. I want you to call this lady and talk to her. See how she feels about you and the idea of marriage. If she's as steadfast about staying single as you told us in the beginning of treatment, we'll have a couple of weeks left to deal with the issue," Bill said as they walked through the cafeteria line, selecting their food.

"I don't know. I was thinking more along the line of surprising her," Jake replied as they sat down on the vinyl-covered chairs surrounding an olive drab, Formica-topped metal table.

"Trust me on this one, Jake. It's not a good time for surprises," Bill stressed.

"Okay, I'll call her," he agreed, without voicing his conviction that no matter what Claire said on the telephone, he *was* going to be her husband. He was sure that God had brought Claire into his life and he was just as sure there was more to His plan. *After all,* he thought, *God could have used anybody or nobody at all if He wanted to get my attention. But he used Claire and Michelle, who need me just as much as I need them. Bill and the group can't begin to understand why Claire doesn't want to marry, and they think it's just about me. They don't realize that she's afraid—not just for herself, but also for Michelle's future.*

"You done eating?" Bill asked while pushing his chair away from the table, the metal legs scraping on the concrete floor. "I've got an alcohol education class to teach in a few minutes."

"Be right with you," Jake answered, carrying his tray across the room and placing the dirty dishes and silverware in the designated bins.

"I should be done with class about two o'clock. Why don't you meet me, and we'll place that phone call," Bill called back over his shoulder as he sprinted up the stairs toward one of the converted classrooms.

Maybe she won't be home, Jake thought as he dialed for an overseas operator, fearing Claire's rejection. It was five-thirty at night in Kansas. She was probably watching *The Tonight Show* or reading a book—Jake hoped it was in a hotel room. His confidence continued to wane as the operator told him his call had been completed and the ringing at the end of the telephone line began to sound in his ear. On the fourth ring he was sure there would be no answer, and his spirits began to soar. But just as he opened his mouth to tell Bill there was no answer, a breathless voice at the other end of the line greeted him.

"Hello. Hello—is anyone there?"

"Claire? This is Jake. Is that you, Claire?"

"It sure is. Were you trying to reach someone else?" she asked, giggling.

"No, only you," he answered while looking toward Bill, who took Jake's cue and exited the room.

"How have you been, Jake? Have you been getting my letters?" she asked. "I didn't know you could make phone calls," she continued.

"I've gotten your letters, and they've meant the world to me, Claire. I hope you'll keep writing—at least for another week or so. I wasn't allowed to call. . ."

"Wait a minute. How come you want me to write only for another week? Are you being discharged or something?" she interrupted.

"I finish treatment in two weeks; then I'm coming back to the States on leave for thirty days. Before you know it, I'll be seeing you again," he ventured.

"I'm sure you've got more important people than me that you want to see when you get home," she replied.

He sensed the hesitation in her voice and felt his throat begin to constrict. "Claire, there's nobody more important to me. I want to marry you." The silence was deafening. "Did you hear me, Claire? I want to marry you—I want us to be a family," he repeated.

"I heard you, Jake, but I told you that marriage isn't in my plans. Remember the conversation we had when we met almost a year ago? You know—the one when we both avowed our intent to remain single?" she asked, obviously uncomfortable with his pronouncement.

"Claire, I know you care for me. Surely you won't deny that," he said, with a note of urgency in his voice.

"Of course I care for you, Jake," she answered in a strained, yet condescending tone.

"Don't patronize me, Claire. You know what I'm talking about. Can you deny what you felt when we kissed?"

"No, Jake, I can't. But a kiss is not the test of whether you love someone, and it's certainly not enough to build a marriage upon. I've continued writing to lend my support while you're going through these tremendous changes in your life. Accepting Jesus is the single most important thing you'll ever do in your lifetime, and giving up alcohol is probably the next. However, marriage to me is out of the question," she told him in a soft voice.

"I would have said giving up alcohol was out of the question six weeks ago, but I've done it. Nobody would have convinced me that I'd ever be so reliant upon God just a short time ago, but I am," he countered, hoping she would at least give him some thread of hope—something to hang onto.

"I hear what you're saying; you *have* made tremendous changes in your life, but. . ."

"But who knows if they'll last, and you're not going to take a chance, right?" he questioned, finishing her sentence.

"You're putting words in my mouth. That's not what I intended to say, but you make a valid point about whether or not I can trust the that changes will last," she said.

Jake had only himself to thank for opening that door and he knew it. Claire wouldn't have voiced her fear that he'd slip back into his old pattern. She'd have been afraid the words would cut too deeply.

"Let me say this, Claire, and then I won't push you anymore—at least not during this conversation. Life holds no guarantees, and people constantly change depending on the circumstances in their lives. Would you agree with that?"

"Yes, I agree we have to adapt to circumstances," she cautiously replied.

"You and Michelle have made a tremendous impact upon my life. Knowing you has made me realize how much I long for a Christ-centered home and a normal life. Hearing how you've learned to accept life's problems, and instead of becoming bitter and turning *against* God, how you've run *to* Him for your protection has made me want to have that same type of relationship. I'm working through anger from my past and looking to God for healing and direction in my life. All

I'm asking for now is that you trust me—give me a chance," he persuasively argued.

"I don't know what to say. I need time to think and pray about this, Jake. The last thing either of us needs to do is make a mistake regarding our futures. I'll make no promises or commitments to you—except to continue praying," she replied.

"I know that a large part of your reaction is due to fear, but I promised I wouldn't push you any further right now. You keep praying. In a little over two weeks I'll be home, and we'll discuss this in person," he said.

"Please don't come here, Jake. Go home to your family instead. That's where you need to spend your time—rebuilding relationships with them," she advised.

"I hear you, Claire," he replied. "Take care of yourself, and give Michelle a kiss for me." He didn't wait for her answer as he slowly replaced the telephone receiver into its cradle.

"Hey, buddy, don't get too down in the dumps," Bill encouraged as he walked into the room. Jake was leaning forward in the chair, his elbows perched on his knees and his face buried between his large hands. "Things will work out—one way or the other—and either way, I *know* you're going to make it."

"Thanks, Bill," Jake replied. "Any chance I could go back to my room instead of that Alcoholics Anonymous meeting?"

"Not a chance," Bill said and then gave him a hearty laugh. "The best thing you can do for yourself right now is get to that AA. meeting. Going off by yourself right now will only be self-defeating. Besides, you've got all night to be alone," Bill continued as he led Jake back toward the small chapel where the twice-daily AA. meetings were conducted.

❧

Claire looked at her watch. It was eleven o'clock, not too late to call Gloria, she surmised as she dialed the telephone.

"You busy?" Claire asked before Gloria had even completed the perfunctory "hello."

"It's eleven o'clock on a Thursday night, and Roger is in the field until next week. Does that tell you anything?" Gloria asked. "What's up? Kind of late for you to be calling."

"I just had a telephone call from Jake, and I needed to talk."

"You want me to come over, or you just want to talk on the telephone?" Gloria inquired.

"He wants to marry me," Claire stated, not answering Gloria's question.

"Oh, I think I'd better come over there to hear this," Gloria replied excitedly. "Put on the coffee pot. I'll be there in ten minutes."

"Obviously you didn't obey any of the speed limits," Claire said to her friend five minutes later as she opened the door. Gloria entered the kitchen, gave Claire a quick hug, and sat down at the kitchen table before the coffee had finished brewing.

"Who's worried about speed limits at a time like this! *What* is going on?"

"I told you—Jake called and said he wanted to marry me," Claire repeated.

"And? What did you tell him?"

"What do you *think* I told him?"

"Yes?" Gloria hopefully ventured.

"Oh, sure! You need to get serious. This isn't some joking matter. Jake's been in rehab for only six weeks now. . ."

"Has it been six weeks already? Seems like only yesterday we were talking about that," Gloria interrupted. Claire gave her friend a look of exasperation. "Okay, okay, I'll be quiet. Please continue," she said, pulling her fingers across her lips emphasize the point.

"He's got two weeks left, and from what I know, he's doing great in the program. However, he seems to think that since he's accepted Christ and given up drinking, all barriers to a marriage between the two of us have been removed."

"And?" Gloria urged.

"And what? There's more to marriage than giving up alcohol and becoming a Christian. You sound just like him!"

"Claire! You're the one who told the guy that you wouldn't consider him because he abused alcohol and wasn't a Christian. You're also the one who continued talking to him on the telephone on a regular basis after you quit dating him. You and Jake know each other better than most married couples. From what you've told me, I don't think there's anything of importance that you two haven't discussed—probably several times and in more depth than I'd even want to think about. Is that true or not?"

"Yes, but. . ."

"But, what? He's measured up to *your* yardstick. Now you're going to change the measurements?"

"Whose side are you on? You're supposed to be *my* friend!"

"I *am* your friend, Claire. But I think when you set up that yardstick, you thought Jake either never would or never could measure up. Now that he's done it, *you're* afraid. Afraid to take a chance, afraid to make changes in your life, afraid to place your trust in God," Gloria sternly moralized.

"You're only making things worse. I expected you to come over here and tell me. . ."

"Tell you exactly what you wanted to hear. Before you send him packing, you'd better get on your knees. As I recall, that's what you're always telling me to do. Don't take his proposal lightly, Claire. You told me that you cared for him and your life had changed since you two met. I also remember you saying that since you'd met Jake you weren't as content with the idea of remaining single," Gloria reminded her.

"You're right. I did say that, and it's true. I do care for him, but I don't know if I love him. Besides, being sober for six weeks doesn't mean that he'll stay that way the rest of his life. You may also recall that I told you I didn't want to settle for someone who could turn my life into disaster."

"Unfortunately, people don't come with refundable warranties, Claire. We could discuss this all night, but I think I'd better get home. If we don't get some sleep, neither of us will earn our pay tomorrow."

Claire walked her friend to the door and then returned to the kitchen and cleared away the dishes, placing them in soapy water before turning off the lights. *I guess it's time I talk to you, Lord,* she thought as she walked into her bedroom and knelt down beside the four-poster antique bed.

fifteen

"Everyone's invited to our quarters for dinner on Sunday afternoon," Bill announced to the members of his group on Friday afternoon. "With graduation next Thursday morning, each of you will either be going home on leave or back to your duty assignments. My wife enjoys entertaining, so it has become a tradition to have my group over for dinner the last Sunday before graduation," he explained. "So bring your appetites, and we'll all have a good time," he told them. "Don't forget there's a trip to a Bavarian clock factory planned for tomorrow afternoon and an AA. meeting tomorrow night. I expect all of you to be in attendance," he called out as the members of the group began to scatter.

Jake was becoming accustomed to having all of his free time planned. Each weekend was filled with compulsory entertainment for the participants in the drug and alcohol program. There were volksmarches through the German woods surrounding the military base, swimming at German pools followed by the steam rooms, traveling to AA. rally weekends, touring through German clock and glass factories, and sightseeing at ancient European castles. Jake enjoyed most of the functions and, coupled with mandatory attendance at AA. meetings twice a day, he had little time to himself.

"Is attendance at your house compulsory?" Nick Soblinsky asked, a sullen look etched on his face and his voice loud enough that those remaining in the room turned around.

"I'd rather think of it as something you'd enjoy attending. However, if you've got a problem, I'll talk to you personally," Bill replied.

"I got nothing to hide from these people. I've been forced

to give them my whole life history, thanks to you. If you give me a choice, I won't be at your house. I've had enough of you to last a lifetime," Soblinsky angrily retorted.

Bill remained calm. "I've got nothing to hide from these people either, Nick. Just thought you might want to talk to me privately. If you don't want to participate on Sunday, you can go with one of the other groups. I think they're going bowling. I'll put you on the list."

Nick nodded his assent and angrily strode from the room.

"What's with him? He's always trying to ruin everything," one of the female group members said to Bill.

"I'm afraid Nick's got a ways to go toward reaching sobriety. Right now he's merely dry," Bill replied. "Don't let his attitude rub off on you guys. We're going to have a great time," he encouraged them. "I've got to get upstairs, and you need to get to your meeting," Bill told those who remained in the room.

❧

"Nick doesn't know what he's missing," Clark Emery stated as he prepared to take another bite of the rouladen and potato dumplings that Bill's wife, Herta, had provided for their Sunday dinner.

"That's for sure," Jake chimed in.

"I'm glad you like it," Herta replied. "Some people don't like German food very well. That's why I made the pot roast too," she explained.

"Looks like we'll be eating pot roast tomorrow," Bill said, giving her a peck on the cheek. "I don't think anybody's touched it."

"Who would eat pot roast when they can get authentic German cuisine like this," Clark retorted as he ladled a dipper of rich, dark gravy over the dumplings he'd just piled onto his plate.

"Don't get too full," she admonished. "I've got strudel for dessert."

"In that case, I'm not even going to consider seconds," Jake replied. "Nothing I like better than German strudel."

Herta rewarded him with a smile just as her daughter ran into the room, dragging a huge doll.

"What have you got there?" Jake asked the towheaded bundle of energy.

"Waggedy Ann," she replied, attempting to hold up the doll that practically overshadowed her small frame.

Jake's eyes riveted toward the mass of red yarn hair adorning the doll's head. "Where did you find that doll?" he asked Herta.

"Oh, I made it for her," she said. "Bill's mother found the pattern at a garage sale and sent it to me. She knows I like to sew. It's become Katarina's favorite," she said, watching as her daughter dragged the doll behind her throughout the house.

"Do you make them for other people?" he asked. "You know, to sell?"

"No, I've never sold one, but I did make one for each of Bill's nieces last Christmas," she explained.

"Is there any chance at all that you could make one for me—before I leave next Thursday?" he asked.

"You two sure are in a deep conversation," Bill remarked as he sat down beside his wife and affectionately placed his arm around her shoulder.

"I was wondering if Herta could make me a Raggedy Ann doll," Jake explained.

"I see," Bill replied, giving him an apprehensive look.

"For Michelle—Claire's daughter. She loves yarn, and I thought the doll might be something she would enjoy," Jake explained.

"Oh, now I really do see," Bill said, obviously understanding why an unmarried soldier would want to purchase an oversized Raggedy Ann doll.

"Jake, I don't know if I could get it done that soon. I may have enough leftover material to make one, but I'm not sure about yarn for the hair and the stuffing," she said.

"Her mind is already planning it out," Bill said, watching his wife's face as she seemed to calculate what needed to be done.

"Let me run upstairs and check," she said, jumping up from the couch and darting off toward the stairway.

"I hope I'm not overstepping my bounds," Jake said. "I just thought. . ."

"It's okay, Jake. She loves to sew and complains that she doesn't have enough to do. If she doesn't really want to make it, she'll tell you. My wife isn't afraid to say 'no' when she doesn't want to do something," he explained.

Herta walked back into the room, her arms filled with fabric. "If you can get me the red yarn and a bag of fiberfill stuffing from the Post Exchange, I've got everything else I need to make one," she told the men. "I'll start on it first thing in the morning. When are you leaving, Jake?"

"Right after graduation on Thursday. I'm catching a plane out of Stuttgart at two o'clock," he said.

"I'll try to have it finished by then," she said, gracing him with an enthusiastic smile.

"I can purchase the yarn and stuffing tomorrow," Jake told her. "I'll get them to you before you leave for home tomorrow afternoon, okay?" he asked Bill.

"Sure, no problem," Bill said as his wife left them to return the supplies upstairs. "You're determined to pursue this woman, aren't you?" Bill asked.

"I know she's the woman I'm supposed to spend the rest of my life with, Bill. I'm sure you don't understand or agree with me, but this is right. I just know it."

"I'm not going to argue with you, Jake. I just want you to get some moral support in place before you get the pins knocked out from underneath you. At least have a plan for yourself if this thing backfires. Let me help you," Bill urged.

"What do you suggest?" Jake asked, knowing in his heart

that Bill was right. The last thing he wanted to do was return to his old habits, and if Bill thought an alternate plan was in order, he should at least listen. After all, Bill was the expert.

"If she tells you 'no,' I want you to have someplace to go. With the exception of Claire and one or two other folks, the only people you consider friends in that town are drinking friends. Am I right?"

"Yeah," Jake answered ashamedly.

"Okay. Then I think if she says 'no,' you need to leave and head for Nebraska. Go visit your mother; get away from the bad influences waiting to destroy your recent success," he counseled. "I don't want you to fail, Jake. So you've *got* to think this thing through and have a plan."

"I know you're right, Bill. I just want to believe that she's going to meet me with open arms."

"Well, chances are that she's not going to do that. I hope she does, but we both know that's not realistic. What do you think about going to Nebraska if it falls apart on you?"

"I guess that would be best. I'd be better off spending my time there. I don't have any drinking buddies up there, but there's sure nothing to do either," he said.

"Come on, Jake. What have we spent the last seven weeks talking about? Take responsibility. You're old enough to get out and find lots of interesting things to do, and I know you've moved beyond the point at which you need someone else planning those things for you. Work on that family genealogy you're always talking about. Go look up some of those long lost relatives and ask their help filling in the blank spaces on that family tree. You'll *all* enjoy it," he advised encouragingly.

"You're right. I'm just looking for excuses to hang around and try to convince her if she says 'no,' but I realize that could lead to trouble," he agreed.

"I knew you'd come around," Bill said, giving Jake a smile and slapping him on the back. "Now, you ready for some of that famous strudel?"

An hour before the graduation ceremony, Jake's excitement began to rise—along with a growing nervousness that he attributed to the impending reunion with Claire. He'd be required to travel in his dress greens since there wouldn't be time to change and pack after the ceremony. Although he preferred traveling in civilian attire when the Army would permit it, that didn't happen too often. Now he was having to forego one of those rare opportunities. *Bad planning*, he thought to himself as he pulled the wool jacket off its hanger and checked his baggage one last time.

"You about ready to check out of our 'hotel'?" Bill asked as Jake descended the stairs into the group meeting room.

"I think so," Jake replied. They were all present and accounted for—all except Nick Soblinsky, who wouldn't be graduating with the group. He'd gone AWOL while the rest of them attended the Sunday dinner at Bill's house the weekend before. The military police had received a call from the local police and had picked him up late Sunday night. He'd gone into town, gotten drunk, and ended up in a brawl. Currently, he was residing in the detoxification center in the hospital.

"We'd better get over to the auditorium," Bill instructed the group. "Wouldn't want to be late for this event. Those of you with families can sit with them or stay with the group, whichever you prefer," he advised.

Once the speakers had completed their part of the program, the graduates were individually called on stage. Instead of a diploma, Bill handed each graduate a marble, advising him to place it in his pocket along with his money. "If you're ever tempted to purchase a drink," he said, "you'll pull that marble out of your pocket when you're ready to pay. Take a long, hard look at the marble and remember where you've come from—use it as a reminder of where alcohol will take you. And if by some chance you go ahead and buy that drink, I suggest that you walk to the nearest door and throw your marble as far as you can. Because as far as I'm concerned, anybody who successfully makes it through treatment and later turns back has surely lost his marbles."

Jake received his marble, which was a white opaque sphere with a small line of red running through the center. He shoved it into his pocket and reached out to shake Bill's hand. That marble was now more important to him than his high school diploma, for it had taken a lot more work and a lot more pain to get that tiny marble. Walking across the stage, Jake noticed Herta sitting near the back of the room. Just as he began his descent down the stairs of the platform, she held up the huge Raggedy Ann doll. He gave her a grin, and little Katarina, who was standing on her chair, waved and pointed at the doll.

"I don't know how you're going to get this on the plane, but I guess that's your problem," Herta said as she handed the doll to Jake after the ceremonies had concluded.

"I know there's no room in my luggage. I guess I'll carry it on board and put it in the overhead compartment," he said. "I hate to rush off, but my ride to the airport is here, and I don't want to miss my plane," he told Herta and Bill.

"You're going to be quite a sight, carrying that thing," Bill said, laughing at Jake as he walked alongside him to the waiting car.

"Take care of yourself, Jake. I'm as close as a telephone, and if there's anything I can do, you give me a call. If you get a free weekend after you're back in Germany, we'd like to have you come back to Stuttgart and visit us," Bill said, pushing aside Jake's extended hand and embracing him in a bear hug. "Keep up the good work, and use that marble to remind you how far you've come," Bill reminded him as they loaded the luggage into the trunk.

"Thanks for everything, Bill. I know you care about each of us, and I appreciate the extra time you've spent with me. I won't let you down," Jake said.

"Don't worry about letting *me* down. Don't let *yourself* down," Bill said and then moved back as the driver of the military vehicle pulled away from the curb.

≈∂

Jake tried to ignore the stares as he walked through the airport and stood in line to board his plane. The red-haired doll was tucked under one arm, and the strap of his carry-on suitcase was cutting into his shoulder. No matter how he positioned the doll, it seemed to be in everyone's way, especially Jake's. *I can't wait to get on the plane and get this doll stowed in the overhead compartment*, he thought as they began to board. Jake was near the end of the line, and when he finally boarded the plane, he handed the stewardess his carry-on suitcase, which he knew was too large to reside under his seat or in the overhead.

"Any chance you can put this with my carry-on?" he asked the stewardess.

"Isn't that a cute doll?" she commented. "No, I'm sorry, only one item per passenger."

Jake nodded. He knew the rule but thought just maybe she'd take it. "Thanks anyway. I'll put it in the overhead."

When Jake finally reached his seat, he lifted the door of the overhead only to find it already brimming full of luggage and personal belongings of other passengers. Dodging in between the other passengers in the aisle, he began checking above the other seats but met with the same results. Exasperated, he finally sat down with the doll on his lap and motioned for a stewardess.

"I can't seem to find any room in the overhead compartments. Could you check further back and see if there's any space available for this doll?" he requested.

"Sure. I'll see what I can do for you," she said, walking away from his seat and checking the compartments as she moved down the aisle.

"Sorry, but there's not enough space left in the overheads

to hold your doll," the stewardess told him, as she returned to where Jake sat.

"You're kidding! What am I going to do with this?" he asked.

"I guess you'll just have to hold it," she told him. "It's always better to pack larger items and send them along with your luggage," she said, giving him a sweet stewardess smile.

"I didn't have time to pack it," he replied. "Any other suggestions?"

"Afraid not," she said. "I'll see if I can find anyone who's willing to 'dollysit' for you."

"Oh, thanks," Jake said, fastening his seatbelt and settling the doll on his lap. "This is going to be a long trip," he said to the soldier sitting beside him.

"You're telling me," the young man replied, pushing the doll's arm out of his lap.

~

"Have you heard anything from Jake?" Gloria asked on Friday afternoon as they were leaving work.

"No, not a word. I did write to him and explained that I still thought it was best if he didn't come to Junction City. He needs to go see his mother, don't you think?"

"It's not me you need to convince, but since you asked, no, I don't think it's his mother he needs to see. I take it you haven't received any conclusive answers from above."

"No," Claire replied. "I wasn't expecting a bolt of lightning, Gloria."

"I know, but I was at least hoping the Lord would soften that hard heart of yours," she retorted, giving her friend a giggle. "When does he get back to the States, anyway?"

"I'm not really sure. Probably in another week or so. He didn't say exactly."

"Since you're not traveling as much, you should be home when he arrives," Gloria teased. "I checked your calendar, and it doesn't look like you're going out of town again until the first of next month."

"Got any plans for the weekend?" Claire asked, wanting to change the subject.

"Roger and I are going to Kansas City tomorrow. We're going to do a little shopping and then stay for dinner. He promised to take me to the movies. There are several new releases, but we haven't decided upon which one to see."

"Sound like you'll be gone until the wee hours of the morning," Claire said. "Hope you have a good time."

"You doing anything?"

"I'm going over to see Michelle, but I'm not sure if I'll go tomorrow or Sunday. Other than that, I don't have any plans. Stop over if you find some spare time," Claire offered.

"Will do. See ya," Gloria replied as she drove away.

sixteen

"Come on in, Gloria. It's unlocked. I don't know why she doesn't just come on in," Claire muttered when the doorbell rang for the second time.

"Why didn't you. . ."

"Hi, Claire."

"What are *you* doing here?" Claire asked in a shrill voice.

"I came back to marry you," Jake said, grinning from ear to ear.

"No. You didn't come to marry *me*! I told you not to come here," Claire retaliated, and without saying anything further, slammed the door. Leaning against the wooden closure, she strained to listen. She couldn't hear any footsteps, yet she was afraid to peek out the small opening in the door. Waiting a few minutes, she had just decided that he was gone when a loud knock sounded. *What am I going to do?* she thought. *I don't know how to deal with this.* Her thoughts were immediately followed by another loud knock.

Gathering all of her courage, Claire pulled the door open just far enough so that Jake could hear her. "I told. . ."

"I'm not going to stand in the doorway and argue with you, Claire. But would you at least open the door far enough so that I can give you this?" he asked, attempting to push the Raggedy Ann doll through the narrow opening. "It's for Michelle. Would you please take it to her?" he inquired.

Reaching her hand through the door, Claire pulled the doll inside. "Thank you. I'll give it to her," she said.

"I'm staying at the Wheatland Inn. Call me if you want to talk," he called as she once again closed the door.

Claire breathed a sigh of relief as she heard footsteps,

followed by the welcome sound of a car motor. Turning, she peeked through the small window in the front door and assured herself that Jake was gone. *Why am I behaving so foolishly?* she thought. But she knew why—it was fear. Fear that if she saw him, if she talked to him, if she allowed him through the door, he would capture her heart. And if he captured her heart, the end result could be painful. Of course, it could turn out to be wonderful, but she wasn't willing to risk her future on that possibility.

"I can't even talk to Gloria," she mused aloud, looking down at the large, red-haired doll that Jake had shoved through the door moments earlier. "And why did he have to go and do this?" she continued, plopping herself on the sofa. "Where did he find you, anyway?" she asked the doll. "Just look at me. I've reduced myself to talking to a doll! Well, why not? At least you won't disagree with my opinions," she said and then laughed at herself.

The large black button eyes stared back at her. "You're pretty cute, you know," Claire said, beginning to carefully examine the gift. A friendly Raggedy Ann smile was embroidered on the doll's face, and her dress was a red print complemented by a white apron. Her legs were covered with the typical red and white striped stockings, ending in jet black shoes. Claire pulled at the back of the doll's dress in an attempt to find a tag or some indication where the doll had been purchased.

"Where did you come from, Miss Raggedy Ann? It looks like you're homemade, but I'm sure Jake Lindsey hasn't taken up sewing," she said, once again conversing with the doll while her hand rested on the doll's head. "Yarn! He bought you for Michelle because she loves yarn," Claire said, embracing the doll. A tear slid down her cheek. *He remembered! Jake Lindsey remembered that my daughter likes to run her fingers through yarn,* she thought as she continued clinging to the doll.

"What am I supposed to do, Lord?" she prayed aloud. "Surely you don't want this man in my life. He's an alcoholic! And even though he says he's accepted you and become a Christian, I'm not really sure he has. What if it's all just an act? And what about Michelle? Making decisions with Glenn about her future was difficult enough; making them with a stepfather would be impossible. I can't jeopardize her future."

Holding the doll, Claire walked to the small table where the telephone sat and looked up the number of the motel. She jotted it down on the small pad beside the phone and then began to dial.

"Wheatland Inn," said the voice at the end of the line.

"Could you tell me Jake Lindsey's room number?" Claire asked.

"Lindsey? Let me see. That's 211. I'll ring it for you," she said.

"No, I don't. . ."

"Hello. Hello. Claire, is that you?" Jake asked. His question was followed by a deafening silence. "Claire, you're the only person that knows I'm in town. Talk to me," Jake urged.

"I just called to say thank you for the doll," she replied and then slammed down the receiver. Her heart was racing, her palms were wet with perspiration, and the knot in her stomach had grown to the size of a basketball. *Now that was really juvenile*, she thought.

"Now what am I going to do? I never should have called," she muttered, when suddenly the phone began ringing. "I just won't answer it," she said, looking at the doll. But it continued to ring—and ring—and ring. *What if Sandra's calling about Michelle*, she thought. *Don't be silly. That's not Sandra; it's Jake*, she argued to herself. *But it might be Sandra. It's not Sandra. You just want to talk to him, so you're telling yourself it might be Sandra. That's probably true, but I can't listen to this phone ring all night. He'll hang up eventually. I don't think so—you know how persistent he can be.* The phone continued to ring as the battle raged within her.

"Hello," she finally answered.

"Finally!" he replied. "I thought I was going to have to listen to that thing buzzing in my ear all night. Why did. . ."

"The only reason I answered the phone was that I thought it might be Sandra calling about Michelle," she responded before he could finish his question.

"I see," he replied, his tone implying that he didn't quite believe what she'd told him. "So if you'd known for sure it was me, you wouldn't have answered? Is that right?" he asked, putting her on the spot.

"Well. . ." she hesitated, "I didn't know for sure, so I can't answer your question."

"Sounds like you're avoiding my question, but I won't press the issue. How's Michelle?" he asked, quickly changing the subject.

"She's doing great. They built a new addition onto the training school and hired full-time physical and activity therapists for the multiply handicapped children. And they're also working on additional integration into the community, so the girls are beginning to attend more functions in the vicinity," she enthusiastically exclaimed. "They're also. . ."

"I'd like to see her," Jake interrupted.

"What?"

"I said, I'd like to see her," he repeated.

"Oh, I don't think that's a good idea. I've already explained that I don't think we should see each other."

"I'd still like to see *her.* You don't object if I go over by myself, do you?"

"I think they prefer that strangers not. . ." she stammered.

"I've already been there by myself, and I'm not a total stranger, you know. Is Sandra still working there? She told me to come visit when I was home on leave," he countered.

"Yes, Sandra's still there, and *I know* you went to visit before you left for Germany. If Sandra's already invited you to come back any time, why are you bothering to ask me?" she asked, somewhat irritated that Sandra had extended him free license to visit *her* daughter.

"Because I'd prefer if you went with me. I haven't seen Michelle for over a year, and the last thing I would want to do is upset her," he explained.

"Then don't go at all. That way you won't have to worry yourself," she retorted.

"I want to see her, Claire. So, either with or without you, I'm going. But I wanted to give you the choice," he calmly told her.

"Well, I don't want you going over there alone, so there's really no choice."

"There's always a choice, Claire, and I'm glad you've chosen to go with me. Any particular time suit you best?" he inquired cordially.

"This is *not* a date, Jake Lindsey, and don't you forget it!" she snapped. "I'll pick you up at one o'clock tomorrow afternoon."

"One o'clock is fine, but *I'll* pick you up," he replied and then hung up before she could say anything further.

&

At twelve-thirty on Saturday afternoon, Jake parked his rental car in Claire's driveway and waited twenty-five minutes before ringing her doorbell.

"You got here nice and early," she said, greeting him at the door.

"Only five minutes," he replied, looking at his watch. "It's nice to see you, Jake. Well it's nice to see you, too, Claire," he mockingly pronounced when she offered no words of welcome.

Ignoring his remark, she picked up her purse and slipped it over her shoulder. "You've been parked in my driveway since twelve-thirty."

"I was afraid you'd insist on driving if I didn't block your car in the garage," he admitted, giving her a grin as he leaned against the door. "You ready?"

"Under the circumstances, I guess I'm ready," she replied, unwilling to give him any leeway.

He gave a mock salute and followed her to the car. "Could we call a truce? Even if it's just for this visit," he asked while sliding behind the wheel of the car and turning his intense blue eyes upon her.

Claire looked directly into those eyes, which she knew immediately was a mistake. Her heart began to race, her mouth felt like cotton, her stomach churned, and her palms were wet with perspiration. She was receiving the confirmation that she had feared: she *did* care for Jake Lindsey—a great deal.

"I suppose we should," she weakly agreed, her mouth so dry her voice cracked. It was as though his eyes were filled with a magnetic force forbidding her to look away. *He can see that I'm falling in love with him*, she thought as he continued to hold her gaze. Her mind began sending out warning signals, but still she was unable to obey. Slowly Jake slid across the seat toward her. His right arm moved along the back of the seat and then descended across her shoulders pulling her toward him while his left arm encircled her waist. His eyes never wavered from hers as he drew her to him. She felt her mouth open slightly as his lips tenderly sought hers, capturing them with an unexpected ardor. As though attached to marionette strings over which she had no control, her arms moved upward around his shoulders while one hand continued to ascend, embracing the nape of his neck as she passionately returned his kiss.

When their lips finally separated, she slanted her head to once again look at him. His eyes remained filled with that same searching intensity she had seen only moments earlier. "Marry me, Claire. You know I love you, and if you'll only admit it, you love me, too," he softly whispered, not yet releasing her from his arms.

"I can't, Jake," she began.

"Why? Tell me why you can't. Is this some self-imposed punishment, or is it that you're setting yourself up as a martyr for Michelle?"

Claire felt herself bristle at his remarks. "It's neither of those things," she said, pulling away from him. "You already know that Michelle's welfare is of primary concern to me, but I certainly don't view myself as a martyr," she vehemently responded.

"You know how I feel about Michelle, and I *hope* you know that I would never try to interfere or go against your will where she is concerned. I'm willing to put it in writing," he offered, his voice taking on a lighter tone.

"It's not just Michelle. You're an alcoholic, Jake, and although you tell me you've accepted Christ, I have concerns about your sincerity. Please don't take that the wrong way," she hastily added. "I certainly can't judge what's gone on between you and the Lord, but. . ."

"Oh, I get it," he interrupted. "It doesn't matter that I've turned my life around, that I've gone through eight weeks of profound self-examination and intense therapy to give up alcohol, or that I've accepted Jesus Christ as my Savior. What you want is someone who never drank and has been a Christian since he was in grade school. Well, there's no way I can do that, Claire, but let me tell you this. People don't come with guarantees. That guy who's been a Christian since he was in grade school may have a crisis in his life and turn away from God. Or, worse yet, turn away from God and toward alcohol. It happens every day!"

"You're being overly defensive. . ."

"No, don't interrupt me. And I'm not being overly defensive; I'm being totally honest with you. I don't *know* that I'll never take another drink. What I do know is that I don't *want* to drink again. As for my Christianity—you're right—that *is* between me and God. I know my heart, and so does God. I'm comfortable with that. So I guess it comes down to this, Claire. I love you; I love your daughter; I've quit drinking and have no desire to go down that road again; I've accepted Christ as my Savior and plan to grow in my Christian faith; and I would very much like to marry you and take care of you and Michelle. But you'll have to trust me."

Before she could speak, he placed his finger across her lips. "Don't answer right now. You give it some thought and a lot of prayer." He removed his finger, lightly kissed her on the lips, and slid back under the steering wheel.

"Hey, where's Michelle's doll?" he asked as he started the car.

"I almost forgot," Claire excitedly cried, jumping out of the car and running back toward the house to retrieve the gift.

Jake smiled as moments later she walked toward him, holding the doll high in the air. "I'm glad one of us was thinking," she said, placing the doll between them on the front seat.

He grinned at her and backed the car out of the driveway. "I'm glad we called a truce," he replied and gave her a wink.

❧

Three weeks later, they stood exchanging wedding vows in the small chapel, with Gloria acting as Claire's attendant and Roger serving as Jake's best man. Michelle sat nearby, the beloved Raggedy Ann vying for space in her wheelchair. Throughout the wedding ceremony, Michelle's fingers ran through the red yarn, busily knotting and tangling the doll's hair, oblivious to the importance of the day's events or the part that she had played in it.

Claire stared deeply into Jake's eyes, looking for any sign she'd made a mistake. *He is a good man who loves me, loves my child, and loves God. We're going to do just fine,* she thought as they pledged their vows.

"I think I *finally* reached one hundred points!" Jake whispered in her ear after the minister pronounced them man and wife.

"I think so, too," Claire replied and met his lips in a lingering kiss.

epilogue

Claire smiled as her husband lifted Michelle into the car, fastened the seatbelt, and placed her wheelchair in the trunk. "How much time have we got?" he asked.

"Thirty minutes," she replied. "Plenty of time," she assured him, although years of marriage to Jake had taught her that unless they were fifteen minutes early, he considered himself late. He had too many years of Army training to change that particular habit, and although she still hadn't adjusted to the concept, they had learned to compromise.

Jake maneuvered the car through traffic to the nearby theater complex and then reversed the earlier process with the wheelchair. "Here we go, girl," he whispered in Michelle's ear, shaking the wheelchair and making her laugh.

Claire followed alongside, and while Jake pushed the wheelchair into the theater, she stopped to purchase the tickets for Walt Disney's *Snow White*, which was once again being offered on the big screen.

"Seems like old times, doesn't it?" Jake asked, as the previews ended and the first scene of the movie began.

"Sure does," Claire replied, watching Michelle's eyes brighten and a smile erupt upon her face as the seven dwarfs began to sing "Heigh-ho, heigh-ho, it's off to work we go."

"We have Michelle to thank for giving us such a timeless movie to keep our memories alive," Jake whispered.

Claire nodded as she settled into her seat and offered Jake the container of buttered popcorn.

৵

Exactly two weeks later, they received the call advising them that Michelle's heart had stopped beating. Although heroic attempts had been made to resuscitate her, they had been unsuccessful.

When they had first received the news, Claire was inconsolable. But Jake, who had been her strength throughout the years of their marriage, proved to be her strength during that first tumultuous year after Michelle's death. When words failed, Jake held her in his arms and prayed, knowing that God would provide, and that the passage of time would temper their grief.

�

Jake sat down beside Claire on the white wrought iron bench and pulled her close. "It's getting colder. You think we should go now?" he asked gently.

She nodded her head but didn't move from the bench.

"Want me to pray with you?" he asked.

Again Claire nodded her head, but she said nothing as he took her hand and held it between his two larger ones.

"Father, we thank You for Your abiding love and faithfulness in meeting all of our needs during this past year as we've mourned for our child and for teaching us that *Weeping may remain for a night, but rejoicing comes in the morning*. We thank You for the years You allowed us to share with her, for the special bond she created in our family, and for her gentle spirit and sweet laughter. We thank You for blessing us with the privilege of rejoicing in the celebration of her life. Amen."

Claire rose from the bench and gave the red and green plaid bow one final adjustment. She extended her arm toward Jake and they walked hand in hand to the car.

"You're quite a guy, Jake Lindsey. Even if you didn't come with a written guarantee," she said as they began their drive home. "Have I told you lately how much I love you?"

"Umm, it's probably been a day or two," he answered, giving her a smile.

"Well, I do love you—very much. And I'm sure glad God sent you my way," she told him.

"So am I, Claire. So am I."

> *. . .weeping may remain for a night,*
> *but rejoicing comes in the morning.*
> PSALM 30:5

A Letter To Our Readers

Dear Reader:

In order that we might better contribute to your reading enjoyment, we would appreciate your taking a few minutes to respond to the following questions. When completed, please return to the following:

Rebecca Germany, Managing Editor
Heartsong Presents
PO Box 719
Uhrichsville, Ohio 44683

1. Did you enjoy reading *A Trusting Heart?*
   □ Very much. I would like to see more books
      by this author!
   □ Moderately
      I would have enjoyed it more if _____

   _____

2. Are you a member of **Heartsong Presents**? □ Yes □ No
   If no, where did you purchase this book? _____

   _____

3. What influenced your decision to purchase this
   book? (Check those that apply.)

   □ Cover   □ Back cover copy

   □ Title   □ Friends

   □ Publicity   □ Other_____

4. How would you rate, on a scale from 1 (poor) to 5
   (superior), the cover design? _____

5. On a scale from 1 (poor) to 10 (superior), please rate the following elements.

___Heroine ___Plot

___Hero ___Inspirational theme

___Setting ___Secondary characters

6. What settings would you like to see covered in **Heartsong Presents** books?_____

_____

_____

7. What are some inspirational themes you would like to see treated in future books?_____

_____

_____

8. Would you be interested in reading other **Heartsong Presents** titles? ❑ Yes ❑ No

9. Please check your age range:
 ❑ Under 18 ❑ 18-24 ❑ 25-34
 ❑ 35-45 ❑ 46-55 ❑ Over 55

10. How many hours per week do you read? _____

Name _____

Occupation _____

Address _____

City_____ State_____ Zip_____

Colleen L. Reece takes girls ages 9 to 15 on nail-biting adven-tures in the Nancy Drew style, but with a clear Christian message. Super sleuth Juli Scott and her savvy friends find love and excitement and learn that it always pays to have a sense of humor.

___*Mysterious Monday*—Julie refuses to believe her father was killed in the line of duty as a policeman. With the help of her new friend Shannon, Julie sets out to reopen the case.

___*Trouble on Tuesday*—Shannon has gotten caught up in fortune telling and an uncanny prediction. In spite of everything her friends try to do, only God can save her from this web of deception.

___*Wednesday Witness*—Being in the wrong place at the wrong time endangers Juli and her friends when they witness a bank robbery.

___*Thursday Trials*—Julie and her friends are called upon to be courtroom witnesses in order to keep the bank robbers from striking again.

___*Friday Flight*—A vacation turns sinister when the girls get involved in an international scheme in Victoria, British Columbia.

___*Saturday Scare*—A leisurely cruise home from Victoria is followed by a horrifying experience on Mt. Rainer.

········· Presents ·········

__HP230 AFTERGLOW, *Irene B. Brand*

__HP233 FAITH CAME LATE, *Freda Chrisman*

__HP234 GLOWING EMBERS, *Colleen L. Reece*

__HP237 THE NEIGHBOR, *Debra Whitesmith*

__HP238 ANNIE'S SONG, *Andrea Boeshaar*

__HP241 DESTINY, ARIZONA, *Marty Crisp*

__HP242 FAR ABOVE RUBIES, *Becky Melby and Cathy Wienke*

__HP245 CROSSROADS, *Tracie Peterson and Jennifer Peterson*

__HP246 BRIANNA'S PARDON, *Gloria Clover*

__HP249 MOUNTAINTOP, *Lauralee Bliss*

__HP250 SOMETHING FROM NOTHING, *Nancy Lavo*

__HP253 A MERRY HEART, *Wanda E. Brunstetter*

__HP254 THE REFUGE, *Rae Simons*

__HP257 TENDER REMEMBRANCE, *Una McManus*

__HP258 THE ALASKAN WAY, *Marilou H. Flinkman*

__HP261 RACE OF LOVE, *Melanie Panagiotopoulos*

__HP262 HEAVEN'S CHILD, *Gina Fields*

__HP265 HEARTH OF FIRE, *Colleen L. Reece*

__HP266 WHAT LOVE REMEMBERS, *Muncy G. Chapman*

__HP269 WALKING THE DOG, *Gail Sattler*

__HP270 PROMISE ME FOREVER, *Andrea Boeshaar*

__HP273 SUMMER PLACE, *Peggy Darty*

__HP274 THE HEALING PROMISE, *Hannah Alexander*

__HP277 ONCE MORE WITH FEELING, *Brenda Bancroft*

__HP278 ELIZABETH'S CHOICE, *Linda Lyle*

__HP281 WILD IRISH ROSES, *Una McManus*

__HP282 THE WEDDING WISH, *Loree Lough*

__HP285 RICH BLESSINGS, *Racine Leonard Davis*

__HP286 A TRUSTING HEART, *Judith McCoy Miller*

Great Inspirational Romance at a Great Price!

Heartsong Presents books are inspirational romances in contemporary and historical settings, designed to give you an enjoyable, spirit-lifting reading experience. You can choose wonderfully written titles from some of today's best authors like Veda Boyd Jones, Yvonne Lehman, Tracie Peterson, Nancy N. Rue, and many others.

When ordering quantities less than twelve, above titles are $2.95 each.
Not all titles may be available at time of order.

SEND TO: **Heartsong Presents** Reader's Service
P.O. Box 719, Uhrichsville, Ohio 44683

Please send me the items checked above. I am enclosing $_____
(please add $1.00 to cover postage per order. OH add 6.25% tax. NJ add 6%.). Send check or money order, no cash or C.O.D.s, please.
To place a credit card order, call 1-800-847-8270.

NAME _____

ADDRESS _____

CITY/STATE_____ ZIP _____

HPS 8-98